ICE INTO ASHES

A DCI JAMES CRAIG NOVEL

JOHN CARSON

DCI James Craig series
Ice Into Ashes
One of the Broken

DCI HARRY MCNEIL SERIES

Return to Evil
Sticks and Stones
Back to Life
Dead Before You Die
Hour of Need
Blood and Tears
Devil to Pay
Point of no Return
Rush to Judgement
Against the Clock
Fall from Grace
Crash and Burn
Dead and Buried
All or Nothing
Never go Home
Famous Last Words
Do Unto Others
Twist of Fate
Now or Never
Blunt Force Trauma

CALVIN STEWART SERIES
Final Warning
Hard Case

DCI SEAN BRACKEN SERIES
Starvation Lake
Think Twice
Crossing Over
Life Extinct
Over Kill

DI FRANK MILLER SERIES

Crash Point
Silent Marker
Rain Town
Watch Me Bleed
Broken Wheels
Sudden Death
Under the Knife
Trial and Error
Warning Sign
Cut Throat
Blood from a Stone
Time of Death

Frank Miller Crime Series – Books 1-3 – Box set
Frank Miller Crime Series - Books 4-6 - Box set

MAX DOYLE SERIES
Final Steps
Code Red
The October Project

SCOTT MARSHALL SERIES

Old Habits

ICE INTO ASHES

Copyright © 2023 John Carson

www.johncarsonauthor.com

John Carson has asserted his right under the Copyright, Designs and Patents Act 1988, to be identified as the author of this work.

This is a work of fiction. Names, characters, places, brands, media, and incidents are either the products of the author's imagination or are used fictitiously. Any resemblance to actual events, locales, or persons, living or dead, is coincidental.

Without limiting the rights under copyright reserved above, no part of this publication may be reproduced, stored in or introduced into a retrieval system, or transmitted, in any form, or by any means (electronic, mechanical, photocopying, recording, or otherwise) without the prior written permission of the author of this book. Innocence is and

All rights reserved

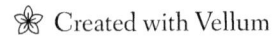

❦ Created with Vellum

*For my daughter Samantha
My biggest fan,
my harshest critic and
my sounding board.
Love you wee pal*

ONE

There was a fairy up in the attic, he was sure of it. She was up here messing about with the gnome, the ugly wee beast with the grotty hair and messy beard. Mind you, the fairy wasn't in much better shape. Straggly hair, tattered dress and a face only a mother could love.

He was sure she was in with the Christmas tree lights, but maybe she had decided she'd had enough of sitting at the top of the tree and had jumped on a bus and left town.

Clark 'Nobby' Brown had been swithering about whether he would celebrate Christmas this year. Ever since his wife, Hilda, had passed four years ago, he had become less enthused as each year went by, and this year was no exception. But he knew Hilda loved Christmas, and if she looked down on him from above, she would be tutting and shaking her head. *What are you waiting for?* she would be thinking, he reckoned. *Get the bloody thing up. December is only a day away and there's nary a sight of any tinsel.*

Now he was up his attic, looking around for the fairy that would sit atop the tree. He'd got the lights down, followed by the tree. In years past, he would pass the bloody thing down to Hilda, who would automatically assume the role of head Christmas tree contractor, and God forbid one of the fragile limbs would break off. He'd managed to get the tree down by himself by tossing it down through the hatch and hoping he didn't break the landing window. A wing and a prayer had worked just as well as Hilda's directions, which involved him sweating and swearing in equal measure.

Then he saw the box with the lid off further along, with the fairy peeking out at him. He could have sworn she wasn't there the last time he looked. Maybe Hilda's spirit was inside the doll thing now, and if that was the case, he would sell the house and bugger off. The only thing the fairy would be sitting on top of would be a bonfire.

She wasn't moving, though, so he could sleep tight. He moved carefully along the wooden boards that served as flooring, knowing every inch of this space.

Then he heard it. A sound, like somebody bumping into something downstairs.

Nobby stood still, listening. The noise hadn't come from up here, he was certain of that. His police officer instinct was still there, although he'd been retired for twenty-five years now, and this instinct was telling him to stay still and listen.

Was it his guest, come back having forgotten something? No, he had locked the front door. He knew he had. It was routine for him.

He stood that way for a good two minutes, which in reality was something quite close to two minutes but could quite as easily have been anywhere from thirty seconds to a minute and a half, depending on when the pain from his arthritis kicked in.

There it was again. A slight noise coming from downstairs somewhere. Nobby knew every creak on the stairs, every groan and moan from the carpeted wood. But it wasn't that.

It sounded like the noise he made when he came in drunk and bumped into the table just inside the front door. The small lamp that lived there was light and bounced about on its base every time he nudged the table. He'd meant to replace it with something more substantial, but he'd also meant to cut back on the drinking and see how that had turned out.

He turned round and overbalanced slightly. A hand that used to be quick and steady reached out blindly and grabbed hold of one of the roof beams. The wood beneath his feet creaked and one of the boards shifted. So much for stealth. Why didn't he just ram a boot through the ceiling below and be done with it?

Okay, the element of surprise was gone, so it would have to be Plan B. No matter what room he was in, Nobby made sure there was some sort of weapon there, something that didn't jump out, like a sword, but could be left lying about inconspicuously, ready for him to pick it up and defend himself with it. The police officer in him again. He'd seen the worst come out in people, and some of the things the bastards could do to other people would make you toss your bag.

A weapon in every room of the house. The attic was the exception. He did have an old tennis racket lying about somewhere, but it wasn't jumping out at him.

He neared the attic hatch and the built-in steps and listened again. Nothing. *Stupid old sod,* he thought. It was probably his imagination running wild. It was windy outside after all.

He walked back, grabbed the fairy that Hilda had loved and walked back to the steps. He threw the unsuspecting figure down onto the landing, climbed onto the steps and pulled the light cord, plunging the attic into darkness. He gingerly climbed down to the landing, Hilda's ghost telling him to be careful, like she'd done every year. It had pissed him off at the time, but now he missed it and would give anything to hear it again.

He put the steps away and picked up the fairy, who was no worse for wear after her flight from above. What Hilda had seen in this monstrosity was beyond him. He was quite sure the dug had got hold of it one year too. Max was long gone, and it was at times like this that Nobby missed him. Maybe he'd think about getting another dug in the new year.

He stood at the top of the stairs, looking at the fairy and then down to the bottom where Max would have stood, gazing longingly between his master and the manky toy he never got to play with, not realising it wasn't a toy but the Christmas tree topper.

Then he felt the fingers on his back, and he gasped, trying to turn round, but gravity had taken hold of him, and he was falling to where Max used to stand.

But Max wasn't there anymore.

TWO

Detective Chief Inspector James Craig walked along the corridor to his boss's office, the headache from the hangover still kicking the inside of his head. He was on leave and wouldn't have had so much to drink if he knew he would be called into the station today. At forty-seven, he thought he could still handle the booze like he could when he was in his twenties, but his body was telling him otherwise.

He rubbed a hand over his close-cropped beard, hoping his eyes didn't look bloodshot like they'd been earlier. He kept his hair short, something less for somebody to grab a hold of in a fight, which happened more and more these days.

He stopped outside his boss's door, about to knock, when he heard the cursing coming from inside. He looked at his watch and shook his head. Barry had started early.

He raised his fist and rapped his knuckles on the door. More cursing followed, before a loud, 'Come!'

Craig opened the door and walked in to find his boss moving a golf putter around in a fashion that was meant to resemble some sort of sport.

'Bastard,' Detective Superintendent Barry Norman said. In Craig's experience, the more the Glaswegian detective got frustrated, the thicker his accent became. It was as strong as the day he'd left Glasgow to head south and join the Metropolitan Police Force, much like Craig himself, although his own journey had started in Fife.

'Good morning to you too, sir,' Craig replied, closing the door behind him. At a little over six foot three, Craig towered over his boss, but what the Glaswegian lacked in height he more than made up for in stature. The boss, too, had a beard, but his looked more like a retired badger, grey with bits sticking out at an awkward angle.

'It's this glass I'm trying to get my balls into,' Norman said, grinning as he turned to look at Craig. 'If you see what I mean.'

'Glad to see the taxpayers' money isn't going to

waste. Just as well it was me coming to your office and not Chief Super Henderson.'

'Henderson is worse than me,' Norman said with a chuckle. 'He was in here the other day and he couldn't hit the ball straight.'

'Must be nice up at the top.'

'It was our lunch break, Jimmy. Everybody has to eat lunch. Or in our case, hit a few golf balls.'

'Handicap getting any better?' Craig asked.

'Not so much my handicap, but my game overall. I'm managing to hit the ball in a straight line now, although my ultimate goal is to get the ball onto the green, or at least somewhere close to it.'

'Talking of goals, have you ever thought about five-a-side football?' Craig said, his face deadpan.

'Too much exercise for my liking, Jimmy. You know me: have a stroll round the golf course with the boys, then get pished in the bar. Much more civilised than running about like a madman, sweating like a P.I.G. just before your heart explodes.' Norman put the putter aside and motioned for Craig to take a seat on the visitor side of the desk.

'Yeah, that's a bit extreme for guys of our age,' Craig said. 'That's why I'm serious about looking after myself now. Watch what I eat, cut back on sugar, alcohol intake down to practically nothing.'

Norman grinned at him. 'You said that last one with a straight face.'

Craig shrugged. 'Two out of three isn't bad.'

'That's what I thought.' Norman sat back in his chair. 'Remember the days when we would keep a half-bottle in a desk drawer?'

'No.'

'Me neither.' Norman reached into a drawer, and for a moment, Craig thought the older man was actually going to produce a bottle and two glasses, but the only thing he brought out was a pair of nitrile gloves. 'Thanks for coming in on your time off, Jimmy. I know you'll be keen to get going to Fife, but I wanted you to see this first.'

He pulled out an envelope and held on to it while holding Craig's gaze.

'If that's two tickets for Eve and me to go on a cruise, I want to say thanks, but we have plans.' Craig saw the other man had dropped his smile.

'It's not your jotters either, so don't worry. But it *is* something for you to worry about. Got gloves?'

Craig nodded, bringing a pair out of his jacket pocket. He always carried a couple of pairs, one for touching possible evidence, the other for threatening his team with a rectal exam if they didn't get a move on.

Norman handed the envelope over and Craig looked at the front. It was addressed to Norman directly, there at the station, and marked private and confidential.

'Open it, Jimmy.'

Craig parted the already opened envelope, knowing that it would have been tested for fingerprints and swabbed.

'No DNA, as you would expect,' Norman said as Craig pulled out a letter and photo. The photo fell onto the desk, face down, and Craig reached out to turn it the proper way up. There was no sharp intake of breath as he saw the image. He was half-expecting it, and if experience had taught him anything, it was to maintain what he called the Duck Principle: calm on top of the water, legs going a mile a minute underneath.

It was a photo of a hammer.

Just like the others.

'When did you get this?' Craig asked.

'Last Friday.'

Craig nodded. Today was Wednesday. He was glad to see that Norman hadn't sat on it and had fast-tracked it through the lab.

Norman sat forward and clasped his hands on

his desk. 'Remind me of how long it's been since you got the last one.'

Craig looked up from the photo. 'One year, two weeks, three days. Molly Sullivan.'

'I remember her. Nice girl. No connection to the others.'

'There never is, boss.'

'Now we have another photo of a different hammer. The lab said it could have been bought in any B&Q. We have CID calling the local stores to see if that particular hammer has been sold recently, but there's been more of them sold than Greggs sausage rolls.'

'Just like the previous times.'

Norman nodded slowly. 'When are you leaving for Fife?'

Craig looked at his watch. 'An hour or so. I was finishing some stuff up in my office first. My wife is already up there.'

'This killer, *The Hammer,* you've been chasing him for five years now and you suspect him of stalking you at times, but you've never had any proof. Just watch your back, that's all I'm saying.'

Craig nodded. 'The usual pattern is to abduct a woman and kill her after holding her for a few days, but there's no discernible timeline between receiving the photo and the actual killing. It ranges between five days and six weeks.'

'That's what I'm saying, Jimmy; he's a clever bastard. The commissioner will be getting his jockeys in a bind, throwing his weight around. I don't know when our boy will strike, but I'll talk to one of your DIs to make him aware,' Norman said. 'Just be extra careful.'

'I will. Is that all, sir?'

Norman shook his head. 'No. One other thing: Olivia. Her dad asked me if you could go and visit her since you're going up to Scotland anyway.'

Craig nodded slowly as images of Olivia Strachan shot into his mind. A late-thirties female living in the psychiatric hospital in Edinburgh. A brilliant psychiatrist, she had been attacked by a patient and left for dead. She had been in a coma for three months and it had taken her more than a year to get over her physical injuries. After her release from hospital, her attacker had come for her again.

The first time, there had been no proof, no witnesses and no physical evidence, and since the attack had happened in her home and not in the hospital, it had been her word against his. And he had been given an alibi by a girlfriend. It was only after the attacker and his girlfriend had split up that the girlfriend came forward and told the truth, that he hadn't been with her at all the evening of the attack.

After the second attack, Olivia's attacker had disappeared and he hadn't been heard from since.

That had been five years ago.

Olivia's father – Callum Strachan – was also a respected psychiatrist and lived in Edinburgh. Originally from Glasgow, he was a friend of Norman's. His daughter had started practising in Fife after she qualified, and this was where the attacks had taken place. Living in the secure ward in Edinburgh made Olivia feel safer now, but not entirely.

Barry Norman had told Strachan that one of his officers originally hailed from Fife and he would be happy to visit Olivia. And Craig had indeed visited Olivia in the hospital, and they had hit it off.

'I'd be happy to go see Olivia.'

'Thanks, Jimmy. It's not true what they say about you.'

'You and I both know it is true.'

'Exactly.' Norman smiled. 'I appreciate you doing that. I visited her earlier this year.' He shook his head. 'What a waste of a life.'

Olivia had been dating a doctor at the time of her attack, and although he had supported her afterwards, he'd gone his own way after she couldn't face life anymore.

'I'd best get going,' Craig said.

'Aye, off you go, son. And don't worry about The Hammer. All of your team are on standby.'

Craig stood up. 'Keep me in the loop, sir.'

But Craig wouldn't need to be kept in the loop by Norman. Somebody else was going to be doing that for him.

THREE

'He was in good shape for his age,' Eve Craig said, sitting opposite the funeral director.

The man was the antithesis of what people expected a funeral director to look like. He was young, mid-thirties, Eve guessed, with a neatly trimmed goatee beard, and he was wearing an immaculate suit with a multicoloured tie, not too gaudy but not too death-ish.

'He looked like it,' Edwin Salmon said. 'If it hadn't been for the fall, it looks like he would have been in good health.'

Eve nodded. 'He was fighting fit. We always kept in touch, and my husband and I would travel up here a few times a year. We emailed and chatted on the phone, and he never complained about any ailment.

Except for having a cold occasionally.' She paused for a moment, caught in her own thoughts. 'He was only seventy-six. He acted like he was thirty years younger.' A tear rolled down her cheek and she wiped it away with a paper hanky.

'I'm sure you have some wonderful memories of him,' Salmon said.

'I do. He was my last living relative.'

'Rest assured we're taking good care of him.' Salmon smiled at her.

'Is there any way I can see him one more time?'

'Of course there is. If you could give me ten minutes or so, I can have him brought into the viewing room where relatives say their last goodbyes.' He stood up and left the office.

Eve sat and stared at one of the prints on the wall. It showed some white houses in Greece. Their son, Joe, was twenty-one now, a student at St Andrews university, but she remembered their holidays to Majorca when he was a kid like they were yesterday.

He had been almost twelve the last time they had gone abroad. When he'd turned thirteen, suddenly it wasn't cool to go on holiday with Mum and Dad. He had relented one time when he was sixteen and had gone to Blackpool with them, bringing his girlfriend with them. James had been strict and had told his son in no uncertain terms that there was to be no hanky-panky. Eve never found out whether there was any hanky or panky, and Joe had never revealed the truth. The girlfriend was history a couple of months later.

Now Joe was twenty-one and studying computer science. She and James had discussed their son's future one night, a discussion that had become heated with Eve telling her husband to go and have sexual relations with himself. Eve had wanted their son to find a safe job, whereas her husband had suggested that Joe attend university and then apply for a fast-track position in the police.

Joe had left London for St Andrews, deciding that living in the moment would suit him for now. That had been three years ago, and with almost eighteen months left of his course, he still hadn't decided in which direction he wanted to head.

Eve jumped, startled by Salmon as he came back into the office.

'I'm sorry,' he said. 'I didn't mean to frighten you.'

'It's okay. I was miles away.'

'Your uncle is ready for you now,' he said.

Eve stood up and followed him out.

FOUR

Craig experienced all four seasons as he booted it up to Edinburgh from London. It was raining when he packed up the Volvo XC90 and topped up at the petrol station. His friend had chastised him for having the diesel. 'Why not?' Craig had said. 'It's not as if we have great-grandkids anyway.' Then Craig had told him where he could shove his electric car. Thirty-three miles to the gallon and a range of six hundred miles he could live with. He reckoned he got off lightly when his journey wasn't impeded by orange-vest-wearing people sitting on the road. Each to his own, that was his motto, but he sighed with relief anyway when he started his journey north.

Sleet, snow and sun, and more rain took turns at battering his car, but he made it to Edinburgh in one piece. It was dark by the time he entered the Royal Edinburgh Hospital car park, hungry, tired and needing a piss.

He sent a text to his friend: *Got to Edinburgh with more than a hundred miles before empty. Hope you're enjoying eating doughnuts while your car is charging. Fat bastard.*

He smiled as he sent it and pulled up the collar of his jacket against the cold evening air. Eve had taken the train from London and asked him if he wanted to do the same, suggesting they could rent a car when they were up in Scotland. But he had said his seats would keep him warm, his music would keep him happy, and there wouldn't be any drunks trying to sit in his lap as they made their way to the train's puking station, generally known to others as the toilets.

He quickly took his phone out again and saw his friend had replied: *Hope you choke on your fucking haggis. Ugly bastard.* He smiled, then fired off a text to Eve: *In Edinburgh. See you soon. Love you. xxx*

Love you too xxx, Eve replied, and he read it on his watch just as he arrived at the door.

He entered the new addition at the back of the old hospital. At the reception desk, he showed his warrant card.

'You're expected, James. I'll have one of the orderlies take you up.' The receptionist smiled as she buzzed him through.

He waited in the corridor, and a couple of minutes later, a female dressed in white scrubs came down to meet him. Nurse Dawn, a young woman he'd met before.

'If you'd like to come with me,' she said, smiling.

It always amazed Craig that no matter what type of hospital he was in, they all smelled the same. Shouts echoed down the corridor from somewhere deep in the building.

'Some of the residents are antsy,' Dawn said.

'It's only to be expected,' Craig said, wondering if some of the patients upstairs should really be in the other part of the building, the one where most of them wouldn't see the light of day again, except through a reinforced window.

They walked up the stairs to the first level and through a set of doors. Unlike the other side of the building, this wasn't high security. Most of the patients either wanted to be in here or were low risk.

There was a ward that had rooms for people who had voluntarily checked into the hospital. They were free to leave at any time and were not considered prisoners. Room 104 housed Olivia.

Nurse Dawn knocked, then opened the door. 'Your visitor is here,' she said, before coming back out. 'Just let reception know when you leave, James. Fire regulations.' She smiled and patted him on the arm before walking away.

The same instruction she gave him every time he came here, not that he'd been many times. He knocked on the open door and walked in, smiling.

'James!' Olivia said. 'Please come in.'

She was standing in the middle of her room, which wasn't insubstantial. It was open plan with a separate bathroom, like a lavish hotel room. It was fitted out with furniture that Olivia had bought over the years until it was almost like an expensive penthouse.

'How have you been keeping?' Craig asked her. Water dripped from his overcoat onto the mat that was just inside the door.

'Let me take your coat; you look sodden,' she said, ignoring his question.

She stepped forward and he slipped his overcoat off and handed it to her. She was close enough that he could smell her perfume, but he wasn't knowledgeable enough on such matters to be able to tell what brand it was.

He stood around like a lemon on his first date,

waiting to meet the parents. It had been a while since he had been here to see Olivia. She hadn't changed much in appearance, except maybe for some lines appearing at the side of her eyes.

She smiled. 'Take a seat, James. I've already hidden the family silver.'

'Pity. I was looking for some good spoons. Oh well, next time.' He walked over to the couch that sat against the back wall, opposite a window that he knew looked onto the back car park. He wondered if she'd been looking out for him.

'Tea?' she asked, walking over to the kitchen area, where the kettle was just going off the boil. That sort of answered his unasked question.

'Thanks.' He didn't remind her how he took his tea; he'd tried that the last time and she'd chastised him gently, telling him she knew.

She poured two mugs and sat down on a chair opposite him, putting the mugs down on the table between them. Almost like the table was an island.

'How have you been since we last talked?' she asked him.

Craig noticed that her mug was within easy reach should she feel the need to use the hot tea as a weapon. Not held in her hand, as that might look like she was on the defensive. Craig had noticed her do the same thing the last time.

And Craig had treated Olivia with kid gloves at first, until she had asked him why he looked like he was balancing on eggs. They had been fine after that, but there were still little signs. He catered to them without fuss.

'I've been keeping healthy. Eve always seems to have a cold all winter, from working with the kids.'

'Still enjoying teaching?' Olivia picked up her mug first and sipped the tea, like she was trying to convince him she hadn't added engine coolant to his.

He mirrored her actions. Once again, the tea was perfection.

'She is,' he replied, putting the mug back down. 'But she's under the weather mentally just now.'

Concern crossed Olivia's face as she put her own mug down, slipping into the role of psychiatrist now. 'Tell me.'

'Her uncle died. Her last living relative.'

'Oh dear. That *is* sad news. I'm so sorry to hear that.'

Craig could tell she was sincere. 'Thank you.'

'Was it sudden?'

'Yes, it was. He fell down the stairs and died of blunt force trauma to his head.'

'That's awful. How old was he?'

'Seventy-six.'

'Not old in this day and age. Tell Eve I send my condolences.'

'Thank you, I will.'

They drank more tea and Craig noticed the rain battering the window.

'My dad told me about you getting another note from The Hammer,' she said nonchalantly.

Normally, MIT didn't discuss cases with anyone to preserve their secrecy, preventing leaks getting out or any information getting into the wrong hands. But Barry Norman had taken it upstairs and had been given the green light to share what information they had about the killer with Olivia. She had dealt with people who had violent tendencies and had gained entry into the minds of some psychopaths. Besides, after five years with no arrests, they were willing to throw the dice and trust Olivia.

'We did,' Craig said, and the thought of the killer about to strike again filled him with dread. And anger.

'It was sent to Barry this time,' she said, sipping her tea. 'Not you.'

Craig nodded. 'That's right. He got it last Friday, and judging by the historical timeline, The Hammer will snatch a female within the next two weeks and kill her within a week. Then he'll dump her body with the murder weapon any time from a day to a month later. We don't know why he does that. But whatever he chooses to do, he'll make the body easy to discover.'

Olivia nodded. 'He's playing games with you, obviously. He's showing you just how clever he is. He can show you in advance what the murder weapon is going to be, and he's giving you a heads-up that a murder is going to be committed. He's extremely confident he's not going to get caught. He's challenging you, James, and so far you've lost every challenge he's thrown at you. That smacks of extreme arrogance. And it shows how much he hates you. If you want my opinion, I think he'll be heading for a final showdown with you one day, but just now he's having a good time, so I wouldn't put money on it being anytime soon.'

'That's very insightful,' Craig said, sipping his tea. 'To be honest, I was thinking the same thing myself. About the showdown, I mean. This is way too personal for it not to happen. It's just a matter of time.'

'He might drag somebody else into it,' Olivia said, drinking her own tea.

'There's been no indication of that in the last five years.' Craig sat back, leaning on one arm of the couch. It was almost as if his body language was daring her to contradict him.

Olivia stood up and walked over to a small dresser and opened a drawer. She took out something that Craig couldn't make out, then she sat back down and handed it over: an envelope.

Craig looked at it for a moment like it was going to lash out at him, before taking it from her. He opened it and took out the contents: a letter and a photo.

The photo, of a hammer, was the same one that Barry Norman had been sent. Craig was about to tell Olivia that she should have given him a heads-up about what was inside, but he let it slide. He took out a pair of nitrile gloves and unfolded the letter.

On it were printed words, and he guessed they'd come out of the same inkjet printer that had spat out the photo.

He read the note:

I know everything that Craig does. I know everybody he knows. Including you. I've studied the man for a long time. I know how he thinks. I know he comes to see you. I know what you'll tell him. I know everything about you too, Doctor. Step outside and I'll introduce you to one of my 'friends'. Claw? Ball peen? I don't know yet. I haven't decided. But I have plenty of time to decide. Or have I?

We'll talk soon, I'm sure of it. And when we do, not even our brave Detective Craig will be able to save you. I'll be there, but you won't know where. Do you have the guts to step out into the world, Dr Strachan?

Until you do, I will keep on killing. You ruined my life, forced me to live a life on the run. So I did what I do best. I hurt people. Not just my victims, but the people who loved them.

Come out and play, Doctor. I'll be waiting. And the winner takes it all. One of us will live to tell the tale. Will it be you? Come out and find out.

The Hammer

Craig read the letter again before folding it up and putting it back in the envelope along with the photo. 'I'd like to keep this,' he said to Olivia as he looked at the postmark. It was stamped Edinburgh.

'He knows about me,' she said, nodding towards the envelope in Craig's hand.

'He seems to know a lot of things,' Craig answered. 'I'm going to have my team in London run your attacker through the system. If it is him, there might be some clues in there.'

'It's been five years, Jimmy.'

'We've been hunting The Hammer for five years. Maybe he knew he couldn't get to you after you came in here, so he started killing other women.'

'Why write to me now?' she asked him. 'You might not know, but I've been going out, under supervision. Not for long periods of time and not every day, but I feel like I should at least try after being in here for years. It did occur to me that he knows about me leaving the hospital. His words about me coming out and finding out could be interpreted either way.'

Craig didn't have the answer. His suspicions about the killer stalking him seemed to have been proved right, if what The Hammer was saying was true; he knew everything about Craig. The fact that he came here to visit Olivia.

'Don't let him put you off. I can call MIT here in Edinburgh and at least have a DC come walk with you.'

'I'd like that. They might not agree, though.'

'I know people up here who could make the call if they don't listen to me. But I'll let you know, and if they agree, you can coordinate with them on a day you'd like to go out.'

'Thank you. But what about Eve's safety?' Olivia asked. 'And Joe's?'

'I'll tell them to be extra cautious. Joe's a big lad; he can handle himself. But this killer is very sneaky.' He nodded and put the envelope in his inside jacket pocket before off taking the nitrile gloves. He took his phone out and called his wife.

'Hello, honey,' she said, her voice bright but not at maximum lumens, which didn't surprise him, considering what she was going through.

'Listen, Eve, I want you to be extra careful until I get there,' he said without preamble.

'I'm always careful,' she said. 'I'm married to a copper, remember? But is there anything in particular I should be extra careful of?'

He was walking a fine line now: tell her the truth and really frighten her, or be vague? Vague it was. 'Just be careful and wary of any strangers. Our boy is about to strike again in London, and it always makes me wary.'

She gave a small laugh. 'I'm in my uncle's house and Finn is here.'

Their German Shepherd barked in the background, like he knew his dad was talking about him.

'Good. Just don't go out and wander about on your own. Take the dog with you.'

'Okay, now you're starting to scare me.'

He laughed, trying to ease the tension. 'Sorry. I just worry about you.'

'Your big boy is here, don't worry. And it's not as if we're staying in a rough area.'

'I know. I'm going to call Joe now, tell him to look out his best shirt for the funeral.'

'His best shirt is one that doesn't have a stain on it. But don't worry, I gave him a heads-up about dressing smartly for the funeral. I told him you'd rent him a suit. I mean, it's not as if you can lend him one of yours.'

'True.' Craig was a big guy, but his son was even bigger. Of course, the lad pumped weights, but he was naturally taller and broader than Craig. That didn't stop him telling his son that if he ever lifted his hand to him, he'd ram an extendable baton up his arse. To which his son had replied that Craig could look forward to the nursing home in his twilight years.

'I'll do my secret rap on the door when I get there,' he told Eve.

'I think Finn will let me know when you're here,' she said, laughing. 'But on the off chance, do your Batman-themed knock.'

'Away, woman. Batman indeed. It's Spider-Man and you know it.'

They said their goodbyes and hung up. Olivia had got up and walked over to the tiny kitchen area and was watching a video on her iPad.

Craig called his son and felt a jolt when the young man didn't answer. He fired off a text, giving him a shortened version of the spiel he'd just given his wife, and was relieved when Joe immediately sent a text back, telling his dad he was having a few pints later with his mates in the centre of St Andrews.

Craig got up and walked over to stand beside Olivia.

'Everybody safe?' she asked.

'Yes. But you knew that, otherwise I would have been jumping up out of my seat.'

She smiled. 'I know. I just wanted to hear it from you.'

'How secure is the hospital, Liv?' Craig asked her. She had insisted on the shortened version of her name the first time they met.

'Pretty secure, I think. I'm not worried, James. I don't go out anywhere and he would have to get past several layers of security to get to me.'

Craig nodded, his mind thinking ahead, envisioning somebody dressed as a doctor being able to worm his way in, or perhaps another visitor. Somebody determined might be able to bypass security.

Obviously, The Hammer had been able to find out about Olivia Strachan and send her the photo and the note. But for what purpose? To scare a woman who was already petrified of her own shadow? He knew there was a connection between Craig and Olivia, and maybe now he was showing off, proving to Craig he could keep one step ahead in the game. Would the killer really target Olivia? Craig couldn't be sure, but at the very least, the killer was making sure it was another thing for Craig to worry about.

One question nagged at him: how did the killer know about Olivia? He hated to think about their being a leak in his department.

'I'll have the letter and photo analysed by the lab. I can make a call to somebody up here and have them look at it,' he said. 'I'll be up here for the next week or so, so don't hesitate to call me if you need me.' He fished out a business card and handed it to her.

She took it and slipped it into the front pocket of her jeans. 'I was thinking about hiring a self-defence expert to come in and teach me some moves,' she said.

'Really? That might be a good idea.'

Craig knew she wouldn't do this. It would mean inviting a stranger into her environment, something she would not be comfortable with. She had said it with the same enthusiasm as somebody suggesting that they try skydiving. It was great sitting in an armchair thinking about it, but taking the plunge was different.

They chatted about books for a little while. Reading was Olivia's passion.

'I have so many books on my Kindle that I'll probably never get around to reading them. But buying them is a compulsion,' she said. 'I see books on BookBub that are on sale and I can't help myself.'

'I read when I get the time,' Craig told her. 'I can't remember what the last one was, though.'

'Why read about crime when you get to live it every day?' she replied with a smile.

He stood up, and Olivia followed suit and walked over to the coat stand. She handed him his overcoat and he slipped it on.

'Thank you for coming,' she said to him, walking forward and giving him a hug without hesitation. There were only two men on this planet she trusted, and he was one of them. Her knight in shining armour, almost. Then she stepped away.

'I'll let you know what we find from the envelope, if anything,' he said.

'I know there won't be anything useful,' she said. 'He's too clever for that. But he knows about me now and that worries me.'

'You'll be safe here, Liv,' he told her.

'I know.' Said without conviction.

'I'll be back before I head back down south.'

'Thank you. I look forward to it.'

She let him out and he heard the lock being turned as he walked away. The room was the closest she would get to the outside world without actually going out into the outside world.

He didn't like the fact that the killer knew where she was and *who* she was.

He stepped out into the cold and dark and walked to his car, not looking back. Not looking up at the window where he was sure Olivia was watching.

He got in and drove away.

FIVE

The drive to Dalgety Bay took forty-five minutes, most of that spent getting out of Edinburgh in the pouring rain. It had stopped by the time Craig left the modern detached house that had belonged to Clark Brown.

Craig had liked the man and had met him on many occasions. Clark was a retired police officer, and he and Craig had often sat and shared war stories over a beer. Craig remembered when Clark and Hilda had bought this place more than twenty years ago. The Bridges was a nice street, and this cul-de-sac off the main road was quiet and upscale. Craig doubted that Clark would have been able to afford this big detached house on his police salary, but Hilda had family money and so they'd splurged.

The headlights picked out Eve's little Volvo XC40 by the front door, and the two windows at the front where two garage doors used to be. A detached double garage was over on the left. Craig parked in front of it, grabbed his two holdalls from the boot and approached the front door to be greeted by Finn barking from inside. The house was a strange place for the dog, so he was obviously being extra vigilant.

Eve opened the door and the dog rushed at Craig when he saw who it was, swishing his tail and rubbing his head against Craig's trousers.

'Don't worry, I remembered to pack a lint roller,' Eve said, smiling at him.

'Come on, boy, let Daddy in to see Mummy.' The dog barked at Craig and ran back inside. Craig stepped inside and kissed his wife. 'I was worried about you,' he said to her.

'I have our boy here,' she said as he closed the door.

Finn looked at her as if he knew she was talking about him. She rubbed his head, which made his tail swipe again.

'Nothing out of the ordinary?' Craig asked his wife.

'You mean apart from my uncle falling down the stairs and dying?'

'Sorry. I meant –'

'No, I'm sorry. I didn't mean to say that. I'm just rattled, that's all.'

He put a hand on her arm. 'Don't worry about it.'

He looked at the staircase in the hallway on the right, imagining Clark lying at the bottom of it. On this floor there were four bedrooms and the bathroom. They had no choice but to go upstairs to reach the living room, kitchen and other rooms.

'It got me the first time I had to walk up them too,' she said as Finn led the way. He had no reservations about going up where Clark had come down head first.

'Let's get a Chinese delivery,' Craig said, slipping his overcoat off. 'I'm sure there's something around here.'

There was. Eve ordered while Craig took a shower. The food still hadn't arrived by the time Craig had towelled off and changed. He went out with the dog, walking him up and down the pavement opposite. He stopped and looked over to the three bridges in the distance crossing the Firth of Forth, looking splendid all lit up in the darkness.

The cold gripped him, so he didn't want to stay out long. He turned to look at the house again. It would have put some people off, spending time in a house where an old man had fallen to his death, but to give Eve her due, it wasn't fazing her.

Craig and the dog walked back inside. He looked at the stairs again, picturing where Clark had lain until he was found. Then the question that had been buzzing about inside his head jumped out.

Who had found Clark dead?

He hung up his jacket, and Eve put Finn's dinner down.

'Who found your uncle?' he asked her just as the doorbell rang; the food had arrived. Finn stopped eating to run at the door with a view to chewing through the wood, and Craig took him back into the living room.

Eve brought the food in and they dished it out in the kitchen before moving to the nook where a little bistro table was set up. It seemed that Clark had liked to sit here and look out over the dark water, to the lights over in Edinburgh.

'You asked who found my uncle,' Eve said as Finn came over and lay down beside them.

Craig nodded, tucking into his sweet and sour.

'His cleaning lady,' Eve said, tucking into her own food.

Craig raised his eyebrows. 'Cleaner?'

Eve nodded. 'After Aunt Hilda died, he couldn't cope with doing all the house chores, so he hired a woman to come in twice a week.'

'How long had he been lying there when she found him?'

'The pathologist said he had died the night before. She found him when she came in to clean. She had her own keys to get in, in case my uncle was out.'

'He must have trusted her,' Craig said.

'Obviously. I don't think he gave her a key right away.'

'I don't recall him talking about a cleaner coming in when we were last up here.'

'Because you two talked about football, drinking and cars. I don't think his cleaner was at the top of his list of topics of conversation.'

'True. But I'd like to talk to her. Just to get her viewpoint.'

'She's upset, Jim.'

'I understand that. I just want to talk to her. And have a look at the police report. One would have been made since it was a sudden death and he was found by somebody. They would have to rule out foul play, which they obviously did.'

'I'll give you her number. There was a little address book I found lying on a coffee table. I remember her name is Delphin.'

Craig was about to ask her if she had read it right, and suggest maybe the girl was called Dolphin, but he didn't want to sound like a smartarse.

'That's a unique name,' he said instead.

'You can ask her about it when you're talking to her.'

'I was going to pop in and talk to some of the old faces at the station in Glenrothes.'

'If they're even still there.'

'Some of them were the last time I dropped in.'

'You should do it then.' Eve pushed her plate away, not quite finished. 'I've been trying to get hold of Mark, but he's not answering his phone.'

Detective Inspector Mark Lawson was Clark's best friend. Lawson was still serving up at Glenrothes the last Craig knew, and was looking forward to retirement so he and Clark could bum about doing God-knows-what during the day. Now, Lawson would be spending his days without his old pal.

'Maybe it's his day off and he doesn't want to be bothered.'

'I've been trying for days. Nothing.'

'I'll ask tomorrow when I go up there.'

They went through to the living room. On the right-hand side was a little sitting area. The windows were semi-circular, like they were in a turret. Two seats and a small table were positioned to make the best of the views across to the bridges and the dark water.

Craig remembered sitting here having a few drams with Clark when they visited. The old man had insisted they stay here in the house instead of using a hotel, and they had sat and chatted and got slowly drunk. Craig sat down in the chair he'd sat in when he was last here. There was a small cabinet over to one side where the bottles of whisky stood. And brandy. And whatever else was the flavour of the month. There was a small silver tray where four whisky glasses usually sat. Two were sitting waiting. Where were the other two?

He stood up and walked over to the cabinet and opened the two slim doors below the bottles, thinking for some reason they might be in there. Clark had taken pride in his house, no doubt aided by the cleaning woman, but he wasn't one to leave stuff around for her to pick up.

The glasses weren't there, but there *was* something that surprised Craig: a bag of lollipops. He hadn't known Clark to have a sweet tooth, but maybe he was a secret sweetie eater. Craig picked up the bag and saw a corner had been cut off. It looked full. Maybe Clark had just snaffled one or two before his death.

Eve had sat down on one of the two couches in the living room, the one facing the large-screen TV. Craig put the bag away and sat on the other couch.

'Are you going to call your brothers?' she asked him.

'Of course I am. I'm just in, so I'll do it in a minute.'

'Excuses. But you need to call both of them.'

Eve picked up the remote for the TV and clicked it on. Craig looked at some of the prints on the wall: seascapes, cottages on the coast. There was even one of the Forth Rail Bridge.

'Hilda must have been worth a few notes,' he commented.

'She played the stock market and left my uncle Clark quite a portfolio. It kept them both comfortable, and they were able to retire in comfort and see the world.'

'Normally, if a copper had this house, they'd be looking into him,' he said, watching as a TV show came on. It was about a small auction house in England where the father and a couple of his grown-up sons went looking for cars to buy and then sell at auction. They were at a house where the owner had three Bentleys of varying ages that had belonged to her now-deceased husband.

'I'd have the red one,' Craig said.

'Stop procrastinating. Call your brothers, then call Joe.'

'Ugh.' He got back up off the couch, then looked at his wife. 'Did you get your uncle's belongings from the funeral director?'

'I did. They're in our bedroom. His personal effects are in a brown envelope. His clothes are in a bag. Why do you ask?'

'No reason.'

'Just the copper in you?' she said, smiling.

'You know me too well.'

He walked downstairs, heading for the master bedroom, flicking on the light switch that put some lamps on. There had to be photos of Clark at the scene, he thought as he stepped into the hallway. He'd ask at the station tomorrow.

In the bedroom, he looked at the padded envelope sitting on top of a dresser and picked it up. He opened it and poured the contents onto the bed.

Clark's watch (a Timex – he couldn't stand the thought of pouring money into something that a mugger would love to get his hands on), a wallet with some cash in it, his house key (Eve always had the spare on her), a metal pen, some coins and one thing that made Craig stare hard.

A lollipop.

SIX

The next morning was surprisingly bright, the December cold held at bay. The sky was blue and Craig watched as a plane came in for its final approach to Edinburgh Airport, seemingly held above the water by black magic.

Eve had left before him, a little after nine. Rob Roy Primary School was in Glenrothes, not far from the police HQ and the MIT, but they had planned on taking their own cars. Eve was meeting her friend Gail, a teacher at the school; she had grown up with Gail and they had never lost touch.

Craig stood holding his coffee, looking out of the living room window as Finn ate his breakfast. When he was done, Craig put his lead on and took him out for a quick walk. This wasn't a through road, so it was quiet. There was a pathway that connected The Bridges with Lumsdaine Drive, but the foot traffic there was mostly dog walkers. He met two of them, nodding a good morning to them both. He stood by the little green area as Finn did his business, and he looked over the cold water to East Lothian.

Finn was done and began to kick up the grass behind him like he was learning landscaping and making an arse of it. Craig didn't know who owned this piece of grass next to the retaining wall, but he picked up after the dog and quickly walked away before some nosy bastard started asking who he was and why his dog was doing its business outside their house.

Craig wasn't in a hurry and his thoughts turned back to *that* day, the day he had almost been killed by a serial killer. A killer Craig had almost caught.

He reflected back on that day, twenty-five years ago. A month after completing probation. He was twenty-two years old and almost didn't make it to twenty-three.

Craig often opened up the Word file he had written, going over events and filling in blanks as he remembered them. Reliving the events over and over in his head.

What if he had done this, or that? Would doing

something different, being late or early, have changed things? Would his father still be alive now? Would things have been different?

He was lucky to have Eve in his life at the time and even more so now. She had helped him through the trauma back then, and when she had said she wanted to go and work in London, he hadn't hesitated to join her, leaving Fife Constabulary for the Met.

His journal of what had happened that dark night had started off with the official report he had written. Then he had rewritten it in his head, not deviating from the official version but making it more personal.

But in the last twenty-five years, he still hadn't changed that one little detail that only he knew about. The detail that might have saved his father's life. Probably not, but there had been the possibility, and now, with his father in his grave for all of those twenty-five years, he would never know.

If there had been some shenanigans the night Clark had died, he wouldn't leave any stone unturned now. He owed it not only to the old man, to Eve and to his father, but to himself.

He went back inside with the dog and walked through to the kitchen with his coffee mug and opened the dishwasher to put it inside. He pulled out the top tray and there they were, two whisky glasses.

A mug sat across from them. He pulled the bottom rack out and saw a few plates in there, with several knives and forks and spoons in the cutlery holder. They were all clean.

He could have used both glasses himself, but that didn't make sense, unless he was lazy. He didn't have a girlfriend that they knew of. That left him having had a friend round, poured them a nip or two each, and then put the glasses in the machine. And since everything was clean, Craig knew that the dishwasher would have washed off fingerprints from the glasses.

A lot of coppers got a gut instinct after a while in the job, and now Craig had one. He wasn't convinced that Clark had fallen down the stairs. However, suspecting it was one thing and proving it was another.

He rinsed his coffee mug and walked to the small study next to the kitchen. It had been years since he'd seen the inside of the room and it surprised him when he saw there was now a lock on the door. The handle had been changed, and Craig didn't know where the key would be kept. He made a mental note to ask Eve about it later.

He went back to the living room, sat down in one of the comfy chairs in the nook, and took his phone out and made a call to Glenrothes MIT. He'd already made an appointment to go up there, but he needed a favour.

'DS Isla McGregor, how can I help?'

'I'm DCI James Craig, Metropolitan Police. I have an appointment to come and see DCS Bill Walker later today, but I was wondering if you would have a phone number for Edinburgh MIT?'

'Hold on, sir, I'll just check.'

He was expecting to hear lift music, something that would make his ears bleed, but instead he got the buzz of noise from an incident room, voices talking at not quite shouting level but getting close to it.

Then the young woman was back on the line. He knew she was young without ever having met her. Talking to many people in interview rooms over the years had honed his perception of voices.

'Here's the number, sir. Got a pen?'

Like he was an old fart who couldn't memorise a phone number when it was read to him. He had the pad and pen beside him just in case. He was daft, but he wasn't that daft.

'Shoot.'

She rattled off the number and he wondered if she was testing his cognitive abilities. It took all of three seconds for him to ask her to read it again, after snatching up the pen.

'It's a bad line,' he said, glad nobody was in the room with him.

Isla read it out more slowly this time, and he could imagine her thinking, *Grandpa.*

'Thanks. I might see you later,' he said.

'I look forward to it.'

'I meant with the others. Not just you and me. With the team when I come up to your place of work.'

'I know what you meant, sir,' she replied, and he could just tell she was smiling, on the verge of laughing at him.

'Good. Well, I'll see all of you later in the station.'

'See you,' she said, hanging up.

Had he come across as an old letch? Christ, he hoped not. Bloody hell. He'd got his string vest in a knot just asking for a bloody phone number. *Good job, Craig. Not long now before Eve will be wiping your arse for you.*

He didn't dwell on it for long. He dialled the

number Isla had given him and got through to Edinburgh MIT.

'My name is DCI James Craig, up in Fife from London. I need to ask a favour.'

'My name is DCI Harry McNeil.'

'DCI McNeil, I'd like to talk about a resident patient at the Royal Edinburgh Hospital.'

'Oh yes? What's up?'

Craig explained what was going on and McNeil said he would deal with it.

'Thanks. I owe you one.'

He hung up and took his laptop out, ready to open up the document that had been saved to so many places, just in case the machine went tits up. He took out the SSD and plugged it into the machine. He clicked on iCloud and found the document he was looking for. *Our trip to Spain.* The file name was meant to make somebody skip on by it should they ever get into his files, but it was unlikely they'd get into this file even if they tried. Not even Eve got to look at this. He hesitated before double-clicking on the document, but then sat back to read it again.

SEVEN

BACK THEN

This is my personal account of what happened on the fifth of November, a month after I received the letter from the chief constable of Fife Constabulary congratulating me on successfully completing my probationary period.

It is almost the exactly the same as the official report, with only a couple of deviations in the truth.

Bonfire Night. Children celebrating a figure from the distant past by setting fire to stuff, not knowing who that figure was, far less caring about him.

But we had more to worry about. Like the old

boy who had been found dead in his kitchen with a knife sticking out of his chest.

I had been first on the scene, and I'd shone my torch through the kitchen window and discovered the man lying on the floor. I was with a uniform called Dan Stevenson, also known by the nickname Desperate Dan. Before we did anything else, I tried the handle of the door (this is the first question CID would ask, smart bastards), but when it didn't turn, I looked at Dan with an unasked question: *You want me to try this or do you want to step up?*

Dan was a big bastard (and maybe still is). I'm not saying he had a penchant for violence or anything like that, but the boy played rugby and didn't take shite off anybody. He'd been on the force for five years, long enough to become jaded but not long enough to step over the line to get booted out. When we needed a battering ram, Dan's size thirteens would do.

This old boy's door was wooden, or else we would have had to resort to Plan B, which was taking out the extendable batons and having at the glass. But there was no need, as Dan booted the lock off with one kick, like he smelled some cow pie inside.

First rule we were taught for when entering what was clearly a crime scene (or somewhere that could possibly be a crime scene) was not to touch anything. But there was a man lying on his kitchen floor with a knife sticking out of him and although doubt flooded through me, I had to check and see if there were signs of life. Dan touched the light switch, using a hanky, and the kitchen was suddenly bathed in a glow from the strip lights above, and I put a couple of fingers on the man's neck, but I couldn't find a pulse.

Now, I was the worst person in the world to ask to check for a pulse on somebody's neck or wrist. I mean, was there one there but so faint I couldn't feel it? Or was I putting my fingers on the wrong spot?

I couldn't see his chest rising and falling, no matter how much I stared at it, and trust me, I stared hard, trying to concentrate on that and not what was clearly a kitchen knife, but there was no sign.

'I think he's gone,' I said, standing up straight.

'Of course he's gone, squire. Look at the poor bastard; if he was any whiter, we would think he's the invisible man,' Dan said, on account of the white tiled floor.

'Aye, he is a bit peely-wally,' I said.

'Fuck me, he left peely-wally behind a while back, Jimmy-boy. That man's stone cold deid.'

'I wanted to make sure. Just for the report, like.'

'Aye, good man,' Dan replied, and I sensed that if

he had been here first, he would have pronounced the man dead by eyeballing him.

I felt like I wanted to wash my hands at that point, but Dan nodded his head sideways, taking his extendable baton out, and said, 'Let's go and check the rest of the house and see if the bastard who did this is hiding.'

He started switching the other lights on.

The adrenaline was coursing through me at this point, so much so that if anybody jumped out, I would have exploded at them. All the self-defence training would have gone out the window and I probably would have head-butted them. But there was nobody else in the house.

Alive.

Later on, we would be told that the second body upstairs on the bed was his wife. When we found her, I could see she had been strangled. She was a frail woman, dressed in a nightie. The duvet had been pulled back, maybe by her kicking and fighting. She lay sideways across the bed, her head hanging limply over the side with the two neckties tied together still round her neck. There were nasty red marks round her neck, raised skin almost the shade of hamburger. Just a bit darker.

We didn't touch anything of course.

'Why don't you put your fingers on *her* neck?' Dan said, and for a minute I thought he was being serious, but then he made a face and shook his head.

'Oh fuck off,' I said to his back as he left the bedroom.

'I'll leave and give you two a few minutes alone.'

Now, I'm all for gallows humour, but there's humour and there's being a sick bastard, and Dan was walking that fine line like a tightrope.

'There's a phone there with the last number she dialled. Looks like yours, Danny-boy,' I said.

'Sick bastard,' he said, making his way down the stairs. 'It's always the fucking quiet ones, eh?'

I didn't have a comeback to that, so I kept my mouth shut, and we waited for CID to arrive, standing in the kitchen, listening to the bangers going off and rockets whistling into the air and exploding.

Dan flicked the light switch back off and peered out past the broken door. 'Don't want to make ourselves a target,' he said, and I wasn't sure if he meant for the killer or the neds throwing fireworks at anything that moved. 'Little bastards,' he said, clarifying.

Then we heard footsteps coming along the flagstones at the side of the house. Dan and I exchanged glances. Neither of us had put away our batons, and I was glad of that. We stepped back into the darkness, and a figure walked past the window and stepped into the kitchen.

'Right, ya bastard!' Dan said as the figure switched the light on.

To give my father – DI James Craig – his due, he didn't flinch but drew a fist back, ready to get in amongst the fray. Then he shook his head at the uniform.

'Skulking about in the dark like some deviant,' he said. He shook his head again as he looked at me.

'There's another one upstairs, sir,' I said. 'We just came down and heard the footsteps. Dan put the lights out so we wouldn't be seen. Just in case he was coming back for something.'

'Good thinking, Constable Stevenson,' my father replied, and gave me a look that said he knew I was lying and we would talk about it the next time we went out for a pint.

'Sir,' Stevenson said, rolling with it. He turned to look at me while my father was looking at the corpse, and winked at me. I didn't need to keep in Dan's good books, but we uniforms looked out for each other.

My father's colleague, an overweight, shorter man called DS Stuart Hunt (shortened to Stew;

nobody knew whether it was a reference to his favourite dish or not), stepped into view and stepped into the kitchen.

'Wee bastard threw a firework at me,' he complained, huffing and puffing and trying not to blow the house down. 'I would have run after him if this wasn't such an important shout.'

Nobody believed the man was even capable of running after a bus, never mind some wee ned who would more than likely turn round and shove a banger up his arse.

'Oh, that looks like it stung,' Hunt said, straight out of Gallows Humour 101. 'Break-in?' he added, looking at the kitchen door.

'That was me,' Dan said, daring Hunt to comment.

Hunt looked at him, waiting for the 'sir' to follow, but came away empty-handed. Dan was taller and wider and heavier than the DS, and he had a look sometimes like his eyes were glazing over.

'No other signs of a break-in then,' my father said.

'Nothing,' I confirmed. 'Front door was locked. So was this one. No windows broken. While we were waiting, we checked the locks on the downstairs windows, and all are locked.'

'He could have let his killer in, boss,' Hunt said, looking over at Dan as if to say, *That's how you address a superior officer*, but he said nothing, and if Dan noticed, he didn't acknowledge it.

'That's what a lot of detectives think,' my father said, 'but what if somebody was pretending to deliver a parcel? They knock on the door asking for a signature and boom, next thing you know they're in the door.'

'That's one theory,' I said. 'Or maybe they were expecting somebody they knew and that person turned round and killed them.'

The other three men stood and looked at me, the newbie in uniform who should be known from that point on as Sherlock Holmes, but the jury was still out on that one.

Hunt raised his eyebrows at my audacity. Two years in and he saw me as a threat to his job.

'Okay then, what else have you got?'

I looked over at him, concerned about the sweat on his face, like his heart was doing irregular things in his chest and he didn't know it yet.

'I think he killed the husband first. That way, he was out of the picture and the killer wouldn't have been overpowered by him, leaving him time to kill the wife easily. I'm assuming they're husband and wife because there's mail on the counter addressed to Mr and Mrs Cairns.'

'Now, let's assume for a second that Mr Cairns knows the killer,' my father said. 'There are two glasses on the coffee table in the living room, both containing what looks like and smells like whisky. Like they were having a friendly drink. One glass is nearly empty, but the other looks like it hasn't been touched, if we assume that a healthy measure was poured but not to the brim. The killer's glass is untouched, leaving no DNA, and I'll bet there are no fingerprints either.'

'Do you think he wiped it before he left?' Hunt asked as more fireworks exploded outside.

I shook my head. 'No. Why wouldn't he just pour it out and put the glass away before he left, making it look like the victim had been enjoying a wee nip by himself? I think the victim poured them both a drink and the killer didn't touch his. But wouldn't your host wonder why you weren't drinking if you were sitting together having a wee gab? I would. I think the killer maybe waited until the drinks were poured, or about to be poured, and excused himself after asking to use the toilet. I checked; there's only one and it's upstairs.

'So, maybe he popped into the bedroom instead

and talked to the victim's wife, Mrs Cairns. She knew him and was comfortable with him being in the bedroom. It was getting on, but it's not like she was asleep. There's a little TV on the dresser opposite the bed, and maybe she was watching TV. Or reading a book. There are books on one side of the bed, the left-hand side as you're looking at the bed. I think that was the woman's side. She was strangled and pulled across the bed to the other side, where she was left with her head hanging over the edge of the bed. Maybe he said something to make her sit up in bed, then put the ties round her neck and pulled her across, choking her.'

'Where did he get the ties?' Dan now asked, getting swept up with my story.

'He got them from a drawer in the dresser where the TV is. It's open slightly and there are ties in there, ruffled up. Maybe he asked if he could borrow a tie? He could have told her that her husband said it was okay and she said, okay, help yourself, they're in the top drawer. He took two out and quickly tied them together. That way he would have more to grip and have more leverage when he was strangling her.'

'Then he came down here, cool as the proverbial cucumber, and decided to stab the husband?' Hunt said, his voice if not quite filled with excitement then hinting that he could see the plausibility of this.

'I think so. Maybe the plan all along was to use the kitchen knife. I get the feeling that the killer was comfortable here, that he had been in the house before and knew his way about.'

I looked across at the knife block sitting on the counter top. I noticed it then, but it didn't register until later on: the lollipop. It was hiding in plain sight right by the knife block, something you wouldn't give a second look. It was only later on that it jumped out at me. But by then it was too late for my father.

'I wonder what the motive was?' Dan said.

'We can ask the neighbours if they know of any friends that the victims had round on a regular basis,' my father said.

Then the forensics crew arrived and the kitchen was buzzing with activity and my father looked at me and Dan. 'Good work. There's a uniformed sergeant out there organising a door-to-door. Go and help him and the others.'

'Yes, sir,' I said.

Dan nodded. 'Yes, sir.' Then he looked at Hunt like he was mentally sticking up two fingers.

Outside, blue lights on the top of patrol cars

flashed through the dark, adding to the colours the fireworks were throwing into the air. A bonfire was still burning in a park further down the road despite the fact time was getting on. A banger went off nearby and a small group of teenagers laughed out loud. Maybe they wouldn't be laughing if we'd taken them into the house and showed them two dead bodies. Or maybe they would. Even back then youths didn't fear the police.

'I thought Tubby McTubster was going to pop a blood vessel or something,' Dan said outside. 'You see him sweating? It was like we told him it was his round. I couldn't let myself go like that. What about you?'

'I want to live long enough to see my grandchildren,' I replied.

'Aye, we want to see retirement, Jimmy-boy. Chunkster will be lucky if he sees next week.'

At that moment in time, Dan didn't know just how prophetic his off-the-cuff remark would turn out to be. Hunt's life was going to be measured in hours rather than weeks or years. But more about that in a minute.

The sergeant was barking orders to the other uniforms, and he waved us over. I moved fast, but Dan moved at a *fuck 'im* speed. *I'll get there when I get there,* he seemed to be saying. The sergeant, an affable bloke who looked like stress was knocking on his door, waiting to deliver a stroke, looked at Dan and obviously decided that he had enough on his plate without calling Dan a gormless bastard and telling him to get a move on.

'Start knocking on doors, that way,' he said, pointing over his shoulder. 'I've got the others going down the street. I don't care if you have to wake them up, I want to know if anybody saw anything unusual.'

'Like setting fire to stuff and setting off explosives in the street?' Dan said.

The sergeant looked at Dan, a big bastard who was obviously mouthy and who looked like violence was simmering just below the surface, and decided which battle to pick, and it wasn't this one.

'Just get a move on, Stevenson,' he said, not wanting to completely relinquish control of the situation.

'Yes, sir,' I replied, and Dan and I started walking along to the first of the houses, just as my father and Stuart Hunt came out of the victims' house, leaving forensics to do their thing just now.

'Right, let's get some of these lazy bastards woken up,' Dan said, peeling off to go up to a door.

It wasn't that late and there were a lot of lights on in living room windows, some residents no doubt woken up by the commotion, if the fireworks weren't enough.

I was knocking on my fourth door when we got a hit. A woman opened the door without hesitation, looking like she was going to come out swinging. She could have been in her forties, or anywhere from there to her sixties. She glared at me, even though she clearly saw the uniform.

'Police,' I said.

'Aye, I can see that,' she said, and I wondered if I was pulling a beamer. 'It's about time you came to my door.'

'I was wondering if you –'

'Come in. I don't want those nebbers to see me talking to you.'

I looked around and saw Hunt looking at me, so at least one person knew where I was. Dan was nowhere to be seen, but that wasn't a problem. Maybe he was inside a house now too, but I wasn't worried about him.

The house was clean and well kept and smelled of polish, almost as if she had been expecting me and had done a quick clean-up.

The living room was empty, and I wondered if she lived alone.

'Do you live alone?' I asked, and her brow knotted.

'Yes, why?'

'I'm here to ask if you saw anything suspicious tonight, and I wanted to ask everybody who lives here.' Beamer part two.

'Just me. And yes, I did. That bastard partially blocked my car in.'

I perked up at that. 'What bast...er, car?'

'What happened at Ronald's house?' she asked me.

'It's an ongoing investigation,' I told her.

'Oh, I see; you want me to give you some information, but you're keeping your cards close to your chest. Well, if that's the case, I didn't see anything.'

Crap. She was being an awkward cow now, and I could see she was obviously the street gossip and was playing games to try to wheedle any information out of me. Did I have a choice? I didn't see I had.

'There's been a murder,' I said.

'Who?' she spat out, taking a step closer to me.

'Who was the guy blocking your car in?'

'I didn't see him. Not closely. He was just a figure.'

'No description?'

'Average build. Wearing a hoodie and a baseball cap. The peak was sticking out the front.' She licked her lips, about to go in for the kill. 'Who got murdered?'

'I'm sorry, I can't say.'

She stood up straight and sucked in a deep breath. 'If that's the way you want to play it, officer, then I can't be of any further use to you.'

I started walking away, heading out the living room, and she watched me get as far as the front door before spilling some more detail.

'I took his number plate,' she said, and I stopped. Turned to look at her. 'Who got murdered?' she asked again.

It would be in the papers the next day and she would find out anyway, so I was prepared to bargain with her, but I still wanted to keep the upper hand. 'What's the number?'

She told me the first two digits and looked at me smugly.

I shook my head slowly. 'They were both murdered.'

Her eyes went wide and her mouth opened. 'Both of them?' Her hand went to her chest. 'Oh my God.'

'Now can you tell me the rest of the number?'

She rattled it off and I wrote it down. 'Thank you. Lock your door. He's still out there.'

I hurried outside and saw Hunt was still over the road, trying to look inconspicuous and not managing very well.

I waved him over.

'We might have our killer,' I said.

EIGHT

Craig stood up from the nook leaving the laptop open. Finn got up with him. The dog was the shepherd and one of the flock was on the move. He didn't care whether his dad was going to the bathroom or not, he was going along for the ride.

Craig rubbed the dog's head below the ear and walked along to the kitchen. It had been a while since he had read his account of that night, and it all came rushing back to him. Of course, the real report hadn't included any of his own observations and opinions, just facts.

Reading about his thoughts on his father felt like a punch in the gut. He missed the old man, missed going for a pint with him. There hadn't been many nights out with his father after that Bonfire Night.

He made himself another instant coffee before going back to the nook. Finn followed and lay down at his feet as Craig looked at the document again. Once again, he was right there, like it was only yesterday.

Back then

'Have you seen your dad?' DS Stuart Hunt said, looking around in the dark. The streetlights were competing with the exploding fireworks to light up the night sky. Groups of people were standing around now, alternating between watching the fireworks and the police walking about.

It was almost ten p.m. and still teenagers and kids were going about like they didn't want the night to end. The fireworks had been going off for weeks and would continue to be shot into the air for weeks to come as their supply slowly dwindled.

'I don't see him,' I said.

'Did you get a name?' Hunt asked me.

'Not quite, but we got a licence plate.'

Hunt looked around again for my father, but

there was a lot of activity in the street with uniforms going about and civilians watching them. Bangers exploded nearby.

The car they had come in was parked close to the victims' house and Hunt strode over to it, telling me to go with him. He opened the driver's door.

'Get in,' he told me, and I got in the passenger seat.

He took his radio out and called the plate number in, and less than a minute later he had an address.

'This might be nothing, so I'm not going to call in the cavalry. We'll go and check it out.'

Falkland was five minutes away from Glenrothes, give or take, depending on traffic and how heavy your boot was. I was thrown back into my seat as Hunt took off, and I looked over at him for a moment, thinking he was having a heart attack and his right foot had somehow jammed itself down on the accelerator pedal as he went into his death throes, but no, apparently this was how he drove with adrenaline shooting through him.

'We'll get up there and have a quick squint around.'

'What if it's him?' I asked. 'Shouldn't we take back-up?'

He snorted and quickly looked over at me before putting his eyes back on the road. 'Back-up? We have batons and you're young and fit. And it'll be two against one if push comes to shove. I'm not worried about it. You shouldn't be either. You heard control; Kevin Robertson is sixty-eight years old.'

'I'm not worried. But even though the guy's sixty-eight, he had the strength to kill two people. Maybe we should have taken Dan.'

'Desperate Dan? He couldn't run fifty yards to a river if his arse was on fire. He might be able to clobber the bastard if we get up close, but we're just going to have a look and see if the car's there. We're not going to go charging in like we're the Light Brigade. If the car's there, we'll get reinforcements up.'

'I hope my dad sees it this way.'

'Look, son, I can stop the fucking car now and you can hoof it back. But one way or another, I'm going up here to see if this geezer went back home after getting his jollies fucking over two people. If he gets away because we were fannying about trying to get teams together, then we'll never hear the end of it.'

It was obvious that his huffing and puffing about pulling over was a load of flannel. I wouldn't have got out anyway, but I was keeping my fingers crossed that my father had got the message from control and he was at that very moment booting up behind us with Dan in the passenger seat. (It turned out he was, but too late to avert the disaster that was awaiting me and Hunt.)

The house wasn't technically in Falkland but outside, up a small road that led to...I didn't know. It could have been the end of the world. But Hunt had the foresight to slow the car down as we turned into the narrow road.

'It has to be along here somewhere. I've been through Falkland many times, so I know it's around here.'

Big, heavy spots of rain fell onto the windscreen, sounding like golf balls. Hunt smiled. 'Let's see the wee toerags firing off rockets in this,' he said.

I had to agree. The rest of the night would be a damp squib. It was as if the sky was a balloon filled with water and suddenly there was a tear in it and its contents had started falling towards earth.

'Going to get soaked,' Hunt complained as the wipers fought a losing battle with the rain.

Through the sheet of falling water, the headlights illuminated an open space over on the left, with a sign that said something about a woodworking school.

'Here we are,' Hunt said, turning in. The lights picked out the car we had been looking for, parked outside the school, itself a long building that looked like it had seen better days.

Over on the right was a house with no lights on inside. Hunt turned the engine off but kept the headlights on so we could see our way.

'I'm going to check the house,' Hunt said. 'Check that place out.' He nodded to the school building. He headed towards the house and I walked over to the woodworking place through the pouring rain, my torch held high in one hand, my truncheon in the other.

We had gone through hand-to-hand defensive training, but I knew if the old bloke came out at me, all that shite would go out the window and I'd just start swinging my baton. As my torchlight cut through the dark and the rain, I grabbed the door handle, but it didn't turn. I walked round the back, looking over to where Hunt had started out, but now I couldn't see him. I shone my torch over to the pathway that led up to the house, which was about five hundred yards away. I thought that maybe he was fitter than he was letting on and had run up to the door.

Round the back of the school, I was out of sight of the house. There was another door further on and I walked towards it, swinging the light about in case the old bastard came out of the darkness. Woods bordered the property, making it all the more dark, if that was possible.

This door was locked too.

That was when I heard it, very faintly.

A scream. Or a yell. I couldn't quite make it out.

I ran back to the pathway and shone my light towards the front door of the house and could have sworn I saw a black-clad figure pulling back out of view as the light hit it.

'Stew!' I shouted. 'Is that you?'

The rain was bouncing off my cap and I regretted not grabbing an overcoat before coming here. We hadn't known the weather was going to turn, but we should have. This was Scotland after all.

The light cut through the darkness as I walked forward. Had Hunt been waving at me to come quickly, gesturing that he'd found something and wanted me to see it? Maybe it was the old man he'd found and he'd overpowered him and wanted me there as back-up, just in case?

I walked up the flagstone pathway. Something that could be called a garden with a great stretch of the imagination was on either side, but it would never feature on the front cover of a home and garden magazine. Weeds had decided to invade the place one day and had battered any flowers into submission. If Kevin Robertson had had a penchant for gardening, it had long ago got up and left.

The front door was open.

'Stew!' I shouted again. *Put a light on, why don't you?* I thought. What if he couldn't? What if Robertson was struggling with Hunt and he couldn't get to it?

He'd got to the door, though, hadn't he?

My heart was racing, the adrenaline pouring through me now, sharpening my reflexes, and I stepped over the threshold into the house, my torchlight cutting through the dark. The darkness seemed so much thicker here, whether exaggerated by the lashing rain or not, I didn't know.

'Stew! Where are you?' I shouted.

Hunt still didn't answer.

I looked back to the road, hoping to see more headlights splitting the darkness, but none came. I thought about calling this in, but what would I say?

My sergeant wasn't answering when I called his name? I'd be laughed out of the canteen.

My torchlight picked out the light switch and I flicked it. Nothing happened. That was why Hunt hadn't put the lights on: he'd tried and found out they weren't working.

Hunt had to be in here somewhere. I'd seen him heading for the house. So why wasn't he answering? The house was old and smelled stale. An 'old man living alone' kind of smell. I moved the torch rapidly around, seeing a staircase over on the right. There was a doorway on my right at the foot of the stairs.

'DS Hunt!' I shouted as the rain thundered off the roof. I shone the light into the room on my right, but there was nobody in it. I gave it a cursory glance before checking the room on the opposite side.

I walked forward, constantly looking back, and then my light picked out the back door leading out of the kitchen. It was open. Had Hunt left that way? Why would he do that without telling me –

My thoughts froze in my mind as I entered the kitchen and shone my torchlight around and saw Stuart Hunt sitting at the kitchen table over on one side.

He had an axe sticking into the top of his head and blood was pouring down his face. His eyes were looking at me, as if begging me to help him, but he was gone. There was nothing I could do to help him, the axe was in so deep.

I swung round, thinking I'd heard something, that whoever had killed Hunt was about to attack me, but nobody was there.

Thunder had started and for a moment I thought fireworks were being let off outside the house, but it was only lightning. It was enough to illuminate the killer running across the back garden. There was an outbuilding on the periphery of the property, sitting right at the edge of the woods. The figure in black ran round the back of it. For a man of sixty-eight, Robertson could move – only it wasn't Robertson, I found out later. He would be found upstairs lying in a blood-soaked bed, killed by the same weapon, they thought, that Stuart Hunt had been killed with.

At that moment, though, I thought it was Robertson, and I raced out into the rain after him. I could have waited for back-up, but how would that have looked? Me standing about twiddling my thumbs as a killer escaped. I went after him, not feeling the rain pounding down on me as I was already dreich.

The back was a lot more overgrown than the front, and the long wet grass tried grabbing on to my trousers. I was surprised my cap stayed on as I ran, but it did, and maybe it was this piece of the uniform that saved my life.

The light from my torch bounced around like it had a life of its own. I gripped my baton with such fierceness that I doubted anybody would have been able to prise it out of my hand at that moment.

I slowed as I approached the outbuilding, which I now saw was an old cottage, obviously not lived in if the manky windows were anything to go by. They were covered in filth, and the grass was growing right up to the front door.

I walked round the side of the old cottage, constantly looking behind me, shining the light. The sky was illuminated by the now constant bursts of lightning and the rain was coming down even harder.

I stopped at the corner, drew my baton back and stepped round, pointing my torch at whatever was waiting for me.

Which was nothing.

Then my world went out from under me. I thought for a second that lightning had hit me, such was the force, but as I went down, I saw the log being tossed to one side. My cap flew off my head, and blood started pouring down the side of my head, but I didn't know it yet. It was being washed away by the heavy rain.

Pain exploded in my head as I slumped against the back wall of the old cottage, and then the figure stepped into view. He was wearing a black overcoat and under the hood was a baseball cap. His face was covered by a dark scarf and all I could see was his eyes, staring at me.

My head was spinning and I was stunned, unable to move as I sat in the pouring rain. Fear gripped me like never before. I knew I was going to die, but I didn't want to think about it.

I couldn't speak, to form words to beg him not to kill me; nothing would come. I only realised I'd been holding my breath when I exhaled.

He had a knife in his hand, and his free hand reached out and grabbed my hair, even though it was short. He twisted his fingers in it and brought my face closer. I just stared into his eyes, not wanting to look at the knife, but he gave me no choice. The blade was brought up to my face, pointing right at my eyeball, getting closer and closer. I tried to move, to pull away, but nothing would function. My arms and legs and everything else was paralysed.

The tip got closer and closer until it stopped. I felt him let go of my hair just as he withdrew the knife. Then I heard a slight chuckle behind the scarf. He was enjoying himself.

'Hey! Ya fucker!' I heard a shout and the unmistakable sound of somebody running towards us, big heavy footfalls running through the brush, torchlight bouncing all over the place.

The killer pulled the knife away, gently tapped me on the face a couple of times then he turned and ran off into the woods.

Everything happened in a blur after that. Voices shouting. People running towards the shaft of light my torch gave off, indicating where I was.

A face near mine. Dan Stevenson. He'd been the one shouting and running. A light shone into my face momentarily blinding me. A quick apology then my father was there next to him, soaked to the skin, kneeling down and holding my head in his hands. Dan had saved me. I felt warm but it was the blood still pouring out of my head.

There was a rush of bodies and it all became too much. I passed out, slumping sideways, my dad catching me. But just before the blackness took hold of me, I thought about the knife that had been near my eyeball. And I knew then with certainty that it hadn't been a knife he was holding.

It had been a small white stick.

I came to realise later that it was a lollipop in his

hand. He was going to ram the lollipop stick into my eye, killing me maybe.

But that didn't go into the official report. I wrote that he had a knife, and that's the way it's stayed for twenty-five years.

Craig stood up from the table, reaching down to close his laptop. Finn got up and he once again rubbed the dog's head. Then he went along to the bathroom and splashed cold water on his face.

He'd thought about the knife/lollipop scenario many times over the years, questioning himself over and over about what he had really seen that night.

He had been admitted to the hospital for three days, and of course when he got out he had to rest at home for a few days more. He had suffered a concussion and was lucky to be alive.

When his girlfriend came in to see him, he had almost blurted out the thing about the lollipop, but would Eve have believed him? He wasn't sure, so he kept it to himself.

He had almost asked his father to go back to the Cairns' crime scene, but didn't.

And that was it. The Cairns, Stuart Hunt, Kevin

Robertson who owned the woodworking school, all murdered by...who? Craig didn't know. They hadn't caught him, and as far as they knew, he was never heard from again.

Until now.

He dried his face and took Finn out for one more pee before heading up to Glenrothes and the police HQ.

NINE

Craig headed along the A921 and cut up past the Mossmorran gas plant to connect with the A92, a trip he had made many times before. It was a cold, damp morning, the last day of November. He reminded himself to take Eve over to the Christmas Market in Edinburgh. Maybe try to get her to go on the big wheel, but he thought she might panic and stand up inside the pod, causing it to start swinging about. Maybe he would just buy her a hot chocolate. Safer that way. Less chance of accidentally getting a kick in the bollocks as she flailed about.

The station on Detroit Road never seemed to change, doing a fair impression of a block of flats in an '80s housing scheme. He parked the Volvo in a visitor's space and went into reception, showing the woman behind the security screen his warrant card.

'Long way from home, aren't you?' she said with a smile. She looked to be in her forties, but could have been older. Craig was never good at answering the question, *How old do you think I am?* He was glad she didn't ask, but if she had, he would have done what he always did in that situation and err on the side of caution. *Twenty-five.*

'I'm originally from Fife. Back for a funeral,' he said, giving her a slight smile back. He didn't want her to think he was happy to be coming back because somebody had died.

'Are you here to see somebody in particular? I'm free for lunch later if you're stuck.' Her grin was wider now.

'Thanks, but I have a busy schedule. I'm here to see DS Isla McGregor. She's expecting me.'

'Here's a visitor's badge,' she said. 'I'd better give you one before you go upstairs.' She slid the badge through the small opening in the Perspex and he clipped it on, ignoring the innuendo.

She laughed and buzzed him through. He opened the door and entered, walking towards the lifts, and he heard the woman say, 'He's a cold drink of water if ever I've seen one.'

Craig smiled to himself, wondering what Eve would say if she knew a woman had been flirting with him. Probably ask him how attached he was to his privates and did he have a sewing kit?

He took the lift to the second floor and stepped out into the corridor where MIT were based. The incident room was further along. He walked up to the door and opened it. He knocked on it as the people in the room turned to look at him, like he was a stranger who'd just ridden into town and had the audacity to come into their saloon.

'You must be DCI Craig,' a young woman said, walking up to him.

'Fifty-fifty chance of being right, and if I wasn't Craig, then no big deal. But you're right. You must be Isla. Is it okay if I call you Isla?'

'It is, sir.' She was tall-ish, around five-eight, Craig reckoned. Blonde hair pulled back into a ponytail, not like a horse's mane but not too short either. She wore black jeans with her shirt tucked in at the front. Craig didn't understand why women were doing that now.

'Come in. I'll introduce you to the others,' she said. He walked in and let the door close on its own, surveying the room, measuring the others up in a few seconds.

'That's DI Max Hold.' Late thirties, looked like he kept himself fit. Smartly dressed.

'Pleased to meet you, sir,' Hold said.

'Likewise, DI Hold.' Maybe first-name terms later for the others.

'DS Gary Menzies.' Late twenties, also smartly dressed, clean-shaven, clearly looked after himself. Not an ounce of fat on the bloke. Maybe cycled to work and was a vegan. But Craig wouldn't hold that against him.

'Sir,' he said, nodding to Craig.

'DS Menzies.'

Isla turned as the incident room door opened and a big man walked in. He was older now, of course, touching fifty if he hadn't already reached it, but the facial features were still the same.

'This is DS –' Isla started to say, but Craig interrupted her.

'Dan Stevenson.' He smiled at the older man and put a hand out.

'Jesus. Look what the cat dragged in!' Dan said, stepping forward and shaking Craig's hand. 'Good to see you, pal.'

'You too.' Craig looked at the man with affection. 'He's the man who saved my life twenty-five years ago.'

He let go of Dan's hand. 'I didn't know you were based here.'

'Aye. Been here a while.'

'We'll need to catch up.'

'We will.'

'And lastly, DC Jessie Bell.'

'Pleased to meet you, DC Bell.'

'You too, sir.'

'I wanted to have a word with Detective Chief Superintendent Bill Walker. We go way back.' Then he had a thought. 'DCI Thompson your boss?' Craig asked Isla.

'Yes, sir. He's on holiday just now. Well, it's more of a recuperation since he got attacked by somebody.'

'Sorry to hear that.' DCI Mickey Thompson was Eve's uncle's friend, Craig knew. They went fishing together, and Thompson wasn't that far off retirement.

'I'll call DCS Walker and let him know you're here.'

'Thanks, Isla.'

Hold walked forward. 'Coffee, sir?'

'Aye, that would be smashing. Thanks. Just milk.'

'No problem.' He walked over towards a table at the back, the unofficial MIT canteen, and switched the kettle on. It must have been on recently because it boiled quickly, but maybe that was just because Craig wasn't watching it.

Hold came over with a mug that had some motif on it, something about keeping calm.

'Thanks,' Craig said, grabbing the mug by the handle.

Isla put the phone down. 'DCS Walker will see you now, sir,' she said. 'Do you know where his office is?'

'Yes. I've been here before.'

They watched him as he turned with his mug still in hand and left the room.

Along the corridor, turn left and there he was, outside Walker's office. He knocked and waited, then entered when the shout came.

'Jimmy!' Bill Walker said, smiling when he saw the DCI. 'Come in. You shouldn't have bothered getting me a coffee. I have a machine thing here that spits stuff out.'

'You wish,' Craig said, sipping the coffee and closing the door behind him.

'Some things never change,' Walker said, shaking his head. 'Grab a pew.'

Craig sat down and put his mug on Walker's desk.

'Dear me,' Walker said, going into his desk

drawer and tossing a coaster at Craig. 'This is no' London you're in now, son.'

Craig grinned and put his mug on the coaster.

'I was sorry to hear about Clark,' Walker said. 'He was such a nice guy.'

'Aye, it was a shock. We were planning on coming up here in a few weeks to spend Christmas with him. Now we're here planning his funeral instead.'

'You never know what's round the corner,' Walker said as Craig sipped more coffee.

'That's true.' He put the mug down. 'I wanted to ask you a favour.'

'Shoot.'

'Hear me out. I'd like to bring one of the officers with me back to Clark's house. Have a wee look around.'

'Are you suspicious of Clark's death? Like it was something other than what was reported?'

'I'm not sure, Bill. You know how we think as detectives. I just want a fresh pair of eyes to look around. To rule anything out.'

'I suppose that could be arranged. Run it by Mark.' Detective Superintendent Mark Baker.

Craig nodded. 'I will. I didn't see him in the incident room.'

'He's probably in his office, skulking about reading the *Beano* or something. I mean, I'm just showing respect for the man by having you ask him, but if he's not happy, he can come and see me.'

'I'll do that. We didn't really keep in touch after my dad died, but he's a good guy.'

'I know he is. If he wouldn't walk about like he has a broom handle up his arse, we'd be fine, but he's a stickler for going by the book. He never gives me any of his guff, though.'

'I appreciate it, Bill.' Craig briefly looked at the older man, who was counting the days to retirement. Police Scotland would lose a good man when he left. He stood up and held out a hand, and Walker stood and they shook. Craig turned and started walking towards the door.

'I'll see you at Clark's funeral,' Walker said.

'Maybe we'll get a nip afterwards. Eve's organising something for after. She's over at the school having a chat with her pal.'

'I look forward to it. Oh, and one more thing.'

'Yes?'

'Your bloody coffee mug, man. Is it the cleaner's day off or something?'

Craig laughed and grabbed the mug, before going back along to the incident room. Mark Baker was there now, obviously having come out from his office, which was located in a corner of the room.

'Jimmy! I heard you were in here, chorying our coffee.' Baker smiled, genuinely pleased to see him.

'One mug and I brought it back.'

Baker came across the room and shook Craig's hand. 'Good to see you again. You should come along to the station more often when you're up here.'

'Usually, Eve has things already planned by the time we get up here.' Craig looked at the older man. 'I was wondering if I could get a look at the sudden death report from the night the uniforms were called out to Clark's house?'

'Of course you can. Isla?' Baker waved the DS over. 'She's one of the best,' he said to Craig in a whisper.

'Yes, sir?' she said, walking over to him.

'DCI Craig needs to see the sudden death report for his wife's uncle. Can you rustle it up for him?'

'Of course I can.'

Craig looked at Baker. 'I was also wondering if I could borrow one of your team for an hour or so.'

Baker raised his eyebrows. 'A wee sesh planned?'

'I wish. But no, I'd like to have somebody else have a look at the scene. A fresh pair of eyes. Somebody who's used to seeing death.'

'Well, why don't you take young Isla here? She's working with Dan, but he can get his head down on the cold case they're working on.'

'Thanks, I appreciate it.'

'No problem. Oh, and Jimmy? Don't go looking in dark corners for the bogeyman. Sometimes, it is what it is.'

'I know.' Craig turned to Isla after looking at his watch. 'Would this afternoon do? I have to meet my wife for lunch and discuss some things for the funeral.'

'That's fine. Call me when you're ready and I'll make my way down there.'

'You know where he lived?'

'DSup Baker dragged us along for a wee party at Clark's. It was his birthday and he thought Clark would enjoy having some company, so a few of us went along for a drink. He was a great soul. I liked him a lot.'

'Great. I'll call you when I'm leaving and I'll meet you there. Eve and I are staying at the house and our dog's there.'

'What kind of dog?'

Baker smiled at her. 'Never mind what kind of dog. Get back to work just now. You'll meet it later.'

Isla smiled and nodded. 'Yes, sir.'

Baker shook his head. 'Maybe we could get a pint at the weekend before you head back down, Jimmy.'

'That would be great. I'm sure Eve won't have anything planned for Saturday. Things are hectic with the funeral.'

'Lunchtime or evening, I'm open. Just give me a buzz.' He took his phone out and held it up expectantly, and Craig took the hint and told Baker his number.

'I have women do this too when I ask for their number in case they try and fob me off with the number for Edinburgh Zoo or something,' Baker said.

He called Craig's number and his phone rang and he put Baker's number in his contact list.

'Right, Jimmy. How long are you up here for?'

'We think the funeral will be next week, so we'll probably leave a week on Sunday.'

'Magic. I'll try calling Mickey Thompson and see if he can join us. He's away to his wee cottage fishing, but God knows what he'll catch right now, except a cold.'

'I think he just likes to get away on his own,' Max Hold said.

'He's probably pished by now,' Baker said, looking at his watch. 'Lucky bugger.'

'Does he know about Clark?' Craig said.

'No. The service up there is sketchy, and I can't get through on his phone. I'll keep trying.'

'I'll let you know about a drink,' Craig said, then nodded to Isla before he left the incident room.

Outside, it was still dull and cold. There was still some time until he was going to meet Eve for lunch, so he called Delphin, Clark's cleaning lady.

TEN

Craig pulled into the school car park just along from the police HQ where he had just been. He took a space near the back of the school, being tracked by cameras.

He got out and walked round to the front door and pressed the buzzer, holding his warrant card up to the camera looking down at him.

'DCI James Craig. I'm here to see my wife, Eve Craig.'

The door buzzed and he walked into reception. The woman behind the counter smiled at him as he approached. 'So you're Eve's husband? We've heard all about you.'

'Good things, I hope.'

'Not one. I for one don't believe the things she said.'

'She must be confusing me with her other husband, the one she sees at the weekends.'

The woman's smile faltered for a moment.

'Just kidding,' he assured her. 'She's stuck with me.'

The door buzzed, just like at police HQ, and he stepped through.

'She's in the staffroom,' the woman said. 'She asked me to tell you. Or was it her other husband? I always get the two of you confused.'

'I guess whichever one of us got here first. But I've never been in this school. I was in the old one before they pulled it down and built this one.'

'Along the corridor, turn right and you'll know which door it is by the smoke coming out of it and the sounds of teachers swearing and maybe crying. Somebody vomiting after having one too many this morning. Oh wait, that'll be lunchtime, which will be happening in' – she looked at her watch – 'five minutes. It'll be like a football match just got out.'

'I'll bear that in mind.'

He followed the directions along the brightly lit corridor, a far cry from the old building he'd visited once, where the corridors played echoes of voices from the past, where the walls had tiles on them halfway up and his shoes had rung out on the floor. It had smelled musty, like dust of old had seeped into the walls and stayed there, permeating the air. This place didn't have tiles on the walls or the floor and didn't have an overpowering smell.

He turned right and was glad to see the woman at reception had been exaggerating about the smoke and puking.

He stopped at the door marked 'staffroom' and wondered briefly if he should knock. *Christ, of course not, Craig,* he told himself. *Bloody knock, indeed.*

He opened the door gently in case there was somebody standing behind it. There wasn't. There were five people in the room, some of them teachers who didn't have a class before the lunchtime bell rang, he assumed.

Eve was standing there talking to her friend, Rose.

'Here he is!' Rose Dempsey said, smiling and holding her arms out. The other three teachers didn't bat an eye, not interested in anything but making the most of their own time.

'Now why can't you be excited to see me like that?' Craig asked his wife.

'I get a backstage pass every day,' she said.

'Oh, come here, you,' Rose said, stepping forward to hug him. He held her and patted her back before they pulled away.

Rose was the same age as Eve and it was clear that she hit the gym like Eve. They were more like sisters than friends. Rose's husband had decided that being married to her was just too much of a chore and he'd left her for a much younger woman. He and Rose had no kids together, but apparently her ex had decided to sow some seeds and had a little boy now. Rose was in a better place now, it seemed.

'How have you been keeping?' he asked her.

'You mean without Romeo in my life? Just peachy. He was dragging me down. I'm glad to be rid of the bastard.' She closed her eyes for a moment, then they sprang open wide. 'My therapist said that the negative thoughts would just take me back to that dark time. Sorry about that.' He smile was falling apart at the seams now and Craig put a hand on her arm.

'It's okay. And it's equally okay to get one off your chest once in a while.'

'Thank you, Jimmy.'

Craig had never liked Rose's ex, Henry Dempsey, entirely. He worked in IT, he had told Craig at a party one night.

'What does that mean?' Craig had asked, three whisky chasers in and at the end of a shitty week. He stood with a beer bottle in his hand.

'It means, I work with computers,' Dempsey said. He too had had a few, more than Craig had, and it showed in the way he swayed slightly on his feet.

'You mean you ask people if they've switched it off and back on again?' Craig said it with a straight face, but another man who'd been standing with them and had come back with a beer bottle burst out laughing.

'That's always the way, isn't it?' Peter, another partygoer, said. 'Forgot to plug the bastard in. I do that all the time.'

'It's a bit more complicated than that,' Dempsey said.

'What? You have to tell them to hit the switch on the wall socket as well?' Peter said, laughing.

'You fucking listen –' Dempsey said, taking a step towards Peter, but Craig put up a hand and intervened.

'Don't you touch me,' Dempsey said, whisky spraying from his lips. 'Why don't you piss off back south where you belong?'

'Take it easy, son,' Craig said, immediately sobering up. 'We're just having a laugh.'

'Laughing at me, though, eh?' Dempsey looked at Peter before walking away.

'We're laughing *with* you,' Peter said. He turned to look at Craig. 'He's a nasty one, that. I don't know what Rose sees in him.' He drank some beer out of the bottle and shook his head at the departing Dempsey.

Now, in the staffroom, Craig looked at Rose and idly wondered what she had seen in Dempsey. Maybe he had shown her his hard drive and she'd been impressed by the size of his gigabytes.

Craig got the image of Rose's ex out of his head.

'We could have dinner one night, if you like,' he said to her. 'What say you, wife of mine?'

'Of course.'

'Oh, you two are busy with poor Clark's funeral arrangements.'

'It's all in hand. Just a couple of other things to take care of. It would be nice to catch up over dinner. You can come to ours if you like. We're staying at Clark's house.'

'If you're sure.'

'Listen to her,' Eve said. 'If you're sure.'

'Of course we're sure,' Craig said. 'We can order in, or I can cook us some steaks.'

'You cook?' Rose asked. She turned to Eve.

'You've been holding out on me. You didn't tell me your husband can cook.'

'He's a man of many mysteries.'

The door opened and a man walked in and smiled widely when he saw Craig and Eve.

'Hey, you two!' Chris Harper said. 'How long have you been up here?'

'A few days,' Eve said. 'For my uncle's funeral.'

Harper slapped his forehead. 'Of course. I'm so sorry for your loss.' He stepped forward and hugged Eve, then turned to Craig and shook his hand. 'Good to see you again, big guy.'

'You too, Chris.'

'How's life treating you down south?'

'Keeping out of mischief,' Craig said.

'Glad to hear it.'

'You're Deputy Head Teacher now, I hear,' Craig said.

'They were looking for the best person to step in and take up the position, but they chose me instead,' Harper said.

'Oh, you know you're the best for the job,' Rose said.

'Aw, shucks.' He laughed. 'Hey, I'll be able to retire a rich man with the pay increase. Not.'

'We don't do it for the money, though, do we?' Eve said.

'Nope. You're right. It's a cliché, but this really is a vocation. I mean, who would volunteer to do this job?'

The bell rang and there was a slight shift in the air. Craig could feel it, like some animals could feel when an earthquake was about to happen.

'Still, it's almost the weekend,' Harper said. 'Good to see you. I'll see you again at the funeral.'

'Good talking with you,' Craig said.

'Can I have a quick word about the fundraiser?' Harper said to Rose, and took her to one of the couches.

Craig looked at his watch. 'I called Clark's cleaner and left a voicemail to see if she'll meet with me,' he said to Eve. 'Then I'm meeting a DS Isla McGregor at the house. I want to get her spin on things.'

'You're not reading something into all this, honey, something that's not there?' Eve said.

'I'm just covering all the bases.'

Eve's smile was gone now as she stepped towards her husband. 'It's bad enough that my uncle is gone. I don't want you thinking that there's something there when there's not.'

He smiled at her. 'I know. I won't.' He had never told her about the lollipop stick that had been mere centimetres from his eyeball.

'Thank you. And I apologise; Rose asked me if we can go for lunch, her and I. We can do lunch anytime.'

'No problem. If Delphin can meet me at the house or anywhere else, that will be great. If she calls me back, that is.'

'Okay. I'll cook tonight.'

'Also, I'll be going over to Glasgow tomorrow to talk to Olivia's father.'

'Do what you've got to do, honey.'

'Catch you later.' He'd started walking away when she called him back.

'Don't I get a kiss?'

All sorts of thoughts ran through his head, like, *Oh yeah, and I'll get the piss ripped out of me*, but it was quicker and easier to give her a peck on the cheek.

'Love you!' she said, but he had turned away and raised a hand.

'Right back at you.'

Then he was out the door.

ELEVEN

It turned out that Delphin lived in Burntisland. She was a bit reluctant to talk to Craig at first, until he could answer her questions about who his wife's uncle was and where he stayed. Only when she was satisfied that it wasn't a scam call did she agree to meet him, but not at her house.

He parked up in the main street and walked into a café called Burger Island. There was a woman sitting on her own with a coffee in front of her and he wasn't sure if it was her or not. She looked the right age, but that didn't help.

'DCI Craig?' she asked, answering his question and saving him from potentially making an arse of himself or possibly getting pepper-sprayed.

'Yes. Do you want a top-up?' he asked her.

'Coffee, thanks. Flat white. And a chocolate chip cookie since you're buying.'

'No problem.'

The woman behind the counter smiled at him. 'So that's one coffee and one cookie. Something for yourself?'

'I'll have the same, thanks.'

'I'll bring them over.'

He sat down beside Delphin. 'Thanks for meeting me.'

'I wish it was under better circumstances.'

He looked at her face, the crow's feet round her eyes, and the skin that looked dry and stretched on her neck. Her eyes looked tired, like she'd seen too much of life. He didn't doubt that she'd had to work hard.

'Aye, me too,' he said. 'We live and work in London, and in all the times we've been coming up here, I never knew you existed. I didn't know Clark had a cleaner.'

'I was with him for a long time. Even before his wife, Hilda, died.' She smiled, but it didn't make her look any less tired, and Craig knew the woman probably worked her fingers to the bone.

The woman from behind the counter came across with two coffees and then went back for the cookies. After she brought them over, Craig spoke to Delphin again.

'How did Clark seem in the weeks leading up to his death?'

'How do you mean?' Delphin asked, breaking off a piece of cookie. Craig thought for a moment that she was going to dunk it in the coffee, but it went straight into her mouth.

'Did anything seem off? Was he worried about anything?'

She washed the cookie down with some of the coffee. 'Do you remember the old days when you would go into a café and ask for a coffee? Not this Americano lark, or a flat white. Just coffee. That's the sort of thing that Clark would worry about. We would sit and have lunch after I did my cleaning work, and he would tell me war stories about the days when he was a copper. He's such a character. Was.'

Craig saw the tears forming in her eyes, and she excused herself and got up from the table. He thought she was going to leave, but she went into the toilet instead.

He sipped his coffee and tried the cookie, waiting for her to come back. When she did, her eyes were even redder than before she left.

'Sorry about that,' she said. 'I still can't believe he's gone.'

'We're the same way. He would let us stay in his house when we came up for a visit. We had some good laughs.' He paused then, looking at her, knowing he had to be careful how he proceeded. 'I want to ask you something. It's going to sound strange, but I have to ask.'

She broke the remaining cookie into pieces and started eating it. 'Fire away.'

'Did Clark ever get death threats?'

Her red eyes widened. 'Death threats? Who would want to harm him?'

'I don't know if anybody would want to harm him.'

More cookie, more drinking her coffee, and Craig noticed her hand was shaking as she lifted the mug.

'If there was, he didn't tell me.'

'Did he have any other friends?' Craig asked, knowing there was DCI Mickey Thompson, but other than that, he wasn't sure.

'Mickey. He's a detective too. Not sure about anybody else. He always spoke about going out drinking with some people, but he didn't say who they were. Coppers, I assumed.'

'When you were there working, did you ever

hear him on the phone arguing with anybody? Anything like that?'

'No. I never heard him arguing with anybody.'

Craig nodded. 'You know he was diabetic?'

'Yes. He had one of those implants on his arm.'

'Did you ever see him eating a lot of sweets? Like lollipops for instance.'

Delphin shook her head. 'No, he never ate sweeties at all. He was good about keeping on top of his diabetes. Why do you ask?'

'No reason.'

They talked about Christmas and the upcoming festivities before getting up to leave. Outside, it wasn't as cold as it looked.

'Thanks for meeting with me,' Craig said.

'There is one thing I remember. From a cleaning perspective.'

Craig perked up. 'Oh? What's that?'

'It's Clark's study. Have you seen it?'

Craig nodded. 'I haven't been in it. What about it?'

'He kept it locked. Most of the time. One day, he was working there and I was upstairs cleaning the bathroom. The doorbell rang and he went downstairs to answer it. When I was finished, I came out and the door to the study was wide open. I was nosy, I have to admit, and had a peek from the doorway. There are corkboards on the walls.'

'Okay,' Craig answered, wondering what she was getting at.

'Those corkboards had newspaper clippings pinned to them. And papers and all sorts of stuff, and it looked like they were about murders. I wasn't bothered because I knew he was an ex-detective. I heard the front door close and went back into the bathroom until I heard him go back into his study.'

'I didn't see any clippings.'

'That's because they're all gone. I found him at the bottom of the stairs and waited for the police to come, then I had to use the bathroom. Police officers were upstairs looking around, and I saw that the study door was wide open and there was nothing on his corkboards. I asked one of the police officers if they had taken stuff from the boards and they said no, and asked what kind of stuff. I said, photos and some bills. They looked at me like I was daft. So, somebody else was in the house and took all the notes about the murder case.'

'Do you remember what case it was?'

Delphin nodded. 'It was from twenty-odd years ago. A detective was attacked in a house somewhere here in Fife. He was killed with an axe to the head.'

TWELVE

Craig drove along the road from Burntisland to Dalgety Bay, thinking about Clark getting a photo of a hammer from The Hammer himself. Delphin hadn't remembered how long before he died he received it, but it wasn't long.

He wondered why the killer had sent it to Clark. But he knew deep down why: it was to get to him, Craig. It was the power game. *I know everything about you.*

He called and spoke to Isla, telling her he'd be home shortly and she could come down any time. She said it would take her maybe twenty minutes with a bit of luck and a prayer.

He opened the front door and Finn was waiting. Craig put the lead on the dog and walked him down the hill a bit from the house. The clouds were gone now, replaced by a blue sky, planes painting a saltire with their contrails. Or 'government chemicals' as Clark used to say, being a conspiracy theorist. He even thought the government was keeping grocery prices too high so old-age pensioners would starve to death and that would save keeping a hospital bed for them. Craig had nodded at this, placating the old man, but then Clark had started in on the butter mountains the EU kept in warehouses, backing up his story. He had hated the EU and everything it stood for, and had cheered when Britain voted to leave, talking about getting rid of the hangers-on. Sometimes his views sounded like those of a demented old man who was trying to buy a one-way ticket to a psychiatric hospital.

'So sorry to hear about Clark,' a woman's voice said from behind Craig, and he was about to swing round, his reflexes sharpened from years of protecting himself, but he turned round and smiled, trying not to give the impression he'd just shat himself.

Finn had noticed her and had stood stock still, no longer panting but laser-focused on her, and if Craig had been paying attention, he would have noticed that. He hoped that he would be paying attention if a man with a hammer came up behind him.

He had seen the woman walking about before. Short, middle-aged, walking with what looked like two ski poles.

'Thank you. It was a shock to us all,' he said, wondering how many times he was going to have to say that in the coming days. 'Do you live close by?' He knew she did, but he wanted to find out which house she lived in without coming right out and asking her.

'Three doors down. I'm Margaret Hamilton. You might have seen me pottering about in the garden when you've come up in the warmer weather.'

'I'm sure I have.' Now it was clear that Clark had told his neighbours about Craig and Eve coming up but had made no effort to introduce them. Craig wasn't disappointed, thinking that the woman was a busybody.

'Nice dog,' Margaret said and that was Finn's cue to rub his head on her.

'He'll get your trousers all hairy,' Craig warned.

'I'm used to it. We had spaniels, but they're gone now. My husband wants to get another one, and we might one day, but not right now.'

'I want to ask you something: have you ever seen anybody hanging around here?' Craig said.

'Hanging around? You mean teenagers?'

'No, I mean anybody acting suspiciously.'

'What makes you ask that?'

Aw shite. Craig hated it when anybody asked him why he was asking questions. He wanted to say, *Because it's my job*, but bit his tongue instead.

'There's a little layby here. Clark mentioned to me on the phone recently that he thought he saw somebody hanging about after dark.'

'He didn't say anything to me, but I'll certainly ask my husband. I'm sure he would have said. Maybe not, though. His head's always in a book these days. Clark might have mentioned it and he forgot to say.'

It was a long shot and Craig shrugged it off, coaxing the dog away from the woman before he got a notion to grab one of her ski poles.

'You should get a pair of these trekking poles,' she said, as if reading his mind. 'You could get fit while the dog got exercise.' Margaret waited for him to confirm that he would indeed get a pair, but nothing could be further from the truth.

'You never know,' he said, not wanting to commit and then have her suggest they go hiking together. 'Anyway, got to shoot. Nice talking to you.'

'Come down and have a cup of tea sometime,' she said, looking at him.

'Thanks, but we're busy with the funeral.'

'After the funeral, then.' Before he had a chance to answer, she was walking away.

Craig crossed the road, looking at the woman's back. Why in God's name would he want to go and have a cup of tea with her and her husband when he'd never spoken to them before? The chances of him socialising with them were slim to none.

He let himself back in, and once he had the dog's lead off, he followed Finn upstairs. While the dog ran into the living room, he went into the study, which wasn't locked now. Lots of push pins and thumb tacks were in the boards, and Craig had wondered what the newspaper clippings were all about that Delphin had seen.

Fifteen minutes later, the knock at the door set Finn off, but Craig calmed him down when he got downstairs to the front door.

'Reception committee waiting,' he said as he opened the door, and to give Isla her due, she didn't look like she had to go home and change. 'Come in. Sorry about Cujo there, but he's the same at home. Doorbell means it's time to play with the UPS man.'

'It's okay, sir. I like dogs.'

Now that Finn saw that this human standing in front of his dad wasn't going to harm him, he started batting his tail about and chuffed a couple of times before turning and hotfooting it back upstairs.

'He's away to find a ball for you to play with him,' Craig said, stepping aside to let her in.

'I'm a Jill of all trades,' Isla replied. 'Catch a murderer, play ball with a dog. You name it, I've got it covered.'

He laughed as he closed the door. 'Can I take your coat?'

She slipped it off and he hung it on the coat rack. 'The living room is upstairs,' he said, then stopped himself. 'But you know that from the parties you came to here,' he said.

'Just one or two,' she answered, climbing the stairs. 'It's not like I'm an animal.'

Craig couldn't confirm or deny either way, so he kept quiet.

'DSup Baker told me that you started your career in Fife,' Isla said as he led her into the kitchen.

'I did my probationary years here, then I left for London. Eve and I were engaged at the time, and a friend of hers told her about a teaching job opening in London, so we talked about it, and she applied and got the job. I transferred to the Met after that.'

He switched the kettle on. 'Tea or coffee?' he asked.

'Coffee, please. Just milk.'

Craig got the mugs ready.

'That was a bit risky, wasn't it?' Isla said. 'If you don't mind me saying so.'

'Asking if you wanted tea or coffee?'

'No, making the move to London with Eve. What if it had gone wrong? What if you went your separate ways? You would have made the move not only to another police force but one in England. It was a huge risk.'

'Have you never taken a risk before, Isla?'

'I have. I took a huge risk too, years ago, and it blew up in my face.'

He wanted to pry and ask her what had gone wrong, but kept quiet. He poured the coffees as she looked out of the kitchen window to the back garden.

'This is a lovely house,' she said.

'It is. Hilda's family had money and left it to her, so she and Clark could afford this house. I think questions were asked upstairs about how he could afford this place, but they were soon slapped down. It's not as if he was on the take, like some people thought, no doubt.'

'It's the business we're in,' Isla said. 'We uphold

the law and are expected to abide by it, but there's always one.'

Craig passed her the coffee after pouring the milk. 'It *was* a huge risk, following Eve down to London, but I knew she was the one for me. If our relationship got blown out of the water, then it would be on her part, not mine. Luckily, it worked out. We came back up here to get married and had a good time with the family.'

'You still have family in the area?' She sipped her coffee.

'My dad died years ago in a car crash. He went off the road and down into the woods and they didn't get to him in time. My brother still lives here, although we don't talk much.'

'That's a shame. I have a sister and we're like twins. Because we are twins.' She smiled.

'Well, I'm not a twin, that's for sure. My brother is a pain in the arse. He blames me for my father's death. He was a detective, just like me, my dad. I miss him a lot.'

'It must have been hard.'

'It was.' He left his own coffee untouched on the counter. 'Anyway, I asked you along here to get your opinion on something. And to help me with something. I could have asked Eve, but she would have got upset with me since it was her uncle who died.'

'Sure. Anything.' Isla put her mug down on the counter top.

'I need you to come with me onto the landing here.'

'Okay.' She followed him out of the kitchen and stood watching as he brought down the extendable ladder from the attic.

'Right, I'm going to climb up here into the attic, and I want you to hide in any of the rooms, whatever one you want, and then when I come down and stand at the top of the stairs, I want you to sneak up on me and push me down the stairs.'

'You want me to push you down the stairs?'

'No, not actually push me, but touch my back, as if you're going to push me.'

'Okay, then. What if I trip and fall and put my hands out and accidentally push you down the stairs?'

He looked at her. 'Good luck with that. I already wrote some letters to be posted in the event of my death if I should be found at the bottom of the stairs, naming you as a suspect.'

'You didn't.'

He nodded. 'Go on. I dare you.' He pointed a

finger at her. 'That's going to make you watch where you put your feet, isn't it?'

'Now I'm tempted to do it and then make it look like an accident. I'll say I came in here and found you like that.'

'Good. Just like they found Clark.' He smiled. 'Besides, there's a nosy old cow down the road who probably wrote your licence plate number down and took a photo, ready to clipe on me to Eve that I had a younger woman round when she was out.'

'I'm sure Eve knows she has nothing to worry about.'

Craig grabbed the ladder and climbed up into the attic and disappeared out of sight.

'Okay, Isla, go and hide now, please.'

When Craig came back and looked down onto the landing, he couldn't see her. He had already noted that there weren't many creaks on the stairs as they had come up to this level. Somebody could have come up here, somebody who had been in the house before and had made a point of noting which stairs creaked.

He climbed down the attic steps and stood on the landing as if he had just been up there looking for something. The ladder had been found just like this when they found Clark. Lying on the landing was an old doll thing that looked like it moved all on its own after dark. What if it had suddenly moved and tripped Clark up?

He shook his head and moved round the ladder and stood at the top of the stairs. He was about to take a step when he felt a hand being placed gently on his back.

He turned round to face Isla, the hairs on the back of his neck standing up. It *was* possible.

'How was that?' she asked.

'Better than you'll ever know.'

THIRTEEN

DCI Mickey Thompson looked out the window into the darkness, watching the rain not so much hitting the glass as pissing against it. For the first time since he'd come up here, he was regretting it. There was no mobile phone service up here in the middle of nowhere.

To make matters worse, there was snow due to come down tomorrow. Previously, the forecast had said cloudy with a chance of rain. He stepped away from the window. Those bastards who worked forecasting the weather needed to go and find another job, making sandcastles or making air bubbles for spirit levels or something. Anything but forecasting the weather. What a bloody joke.

Darkness had come down with a vengeance as

usual. Just as well the power hadn't gone out, or else he'd have had to walk a couple of miles into the village just to get a warm-up and a pint. He had the gas tank heater, mind, but that was only for reserve or the middle of the night. Why pay for your own heat when you could scrounge it off the landlord in the pub for free?

He chuckled. He couldn't wait for his old mate Clark to join him like they had planned. He had said he wouldn't be able to make it right away when Thompson suggested they go fishing. But catching fish was the last thing on their minds; there were a couple of women in the village who they got on with really well, and of course there was the drinking. They couldn't tell the others that this was the reason they were coming up to Thompson's cottage. Fishing sounded better, and those who weren't interested in the sport got bored and didn't ask any more questions.

Thompson wanted to call his friend, but not having any service was a bastard out here. Though it meant Thompson couldn't be called back to work, so it had its advantages.

He went through to the kitchen, thinking that he'd make himself a coffee. Of course they'd have a wee sesh when Clark got here, but they wouldn't get blootered. That was what the upcoming weekend was for, but it was only Thursday.

He switched the kettle on and turned the radio on. Listening to the radio was a lost art, he thought. Kids nowadays were more interested in watching videos of cats skelping dogs, or drunk people falling on their arse. Thompson chuckled. Some of those bloody cats were funny, though, he had to admit –

He heard the front door open and close again.

He hadn't heard the car come up the rough driveway, but then again, a jumbo jet could land in the front garden and he wouldn't hear it for that fucking wind. He was going to write a strong letter to the BBC weather department and tell the guy who was on the six o'clock news that he needed to retire.

Maybe his friend had decided to come up earlier than expected. Brilliant.

He walked through to the living room, where the front door was. 'Glad you could make it, mucker,' he said. *What the hell?* Clark had left the front door open. The wind was shoving the rain in almost horizontally. 'What the hell, Clark? Are you pished already?'

No answer as Thompson walked forward and quickly closed the door, trying not to get soaked. He turned round as he heard a noise coming from upstairs.

'Nobby? That you?'

No answer. Christ, had he come in soaked and nashed upstairs to dry off? He walked back over to the front door and opened it, immediately getting pelted with wind and rain, and he looked out into his driveway. He switched the outside light on but didn't see a car. Had the stupid sod parked further down and walked? Why would he do that? He shut the door again, the front of his sweater and trousers now wet with the rain.

'Fuck's sake, Nobby, are you up there?'

Still no answer. Thompson shook his head and began climbing the stairs to the top floor, where the bathroom and two bedrooms were. He noticed wet, muddy footprints on the carpet, which wasn't brand new but wasn't threadbare either.

'Couldn't take your boots off at the door, could you?' he said in a low voice.

Clark's bedroom door was open and the light was on.

'Cat got your tongue?' he said, walking along the landing, expecting his pal to come bounding out, but no, there was no sound. 'Nobby? You in there, pal? You okay?'

Thompson knocked on the door and it swung open. The room was a decent size with a bed, drawers and a wardrobe. Not the Sheraton, but warm and comfortable.

There was nobody in there. Maybe it was his imagination.

He went back downstairs and into the kitchen. He smiled, then took one of the knives out of the block.

One of the big ones.

FOURTEEN

Eve was sitting with a glass of wine while Craig made do with a coffee. He'd long ago built up a tolerance for caffeine, even though his bladder would disagree at two in the morning.

He had thanked Isla earlier, and she had left without asking him too many questions, like, *Who do you think offed the old man?* He didn't want to ask Eve now if she would be open to the idea that somebody had pushed her uncle down the stairs. He would leave that until after the funeral.

'It was good seeing Rose and Chris today,' he said.

Eve had a magazine on her lap and the dog lying next to her on the couch. 'It was. She seems so much happier now that Henry is out of her life.'

'He was a moody sod, but then again, maybe he was stressed out. Nobody knew what was going on behind closed doors. Maybe they were fighting a lot. That doesn't do anybody any good.'

'She didn't go into a lot of details at the time, but she did say things were getting rough.'

'Either way, she had a lucky escape.'

'I don't know what that girl saw in him.'

'Which one?'

'The one he ran away with. Eliza Banfield. She worked at the vet's that Rose and Henry used. They took their cat there and I guess she caught his eye.'

'You never know, do you?' Craig said.

Eve looked at him. 'What do you mean? Have you been eying up women at work or something?'

He laughed. 'No. I meant if you're that way inclined. And Henry Dempsey was. Maybe it was inevitable that he was going to meet somebody else. I'm not that way inclined at all. I'm quite happy with my woman.'

'I'm your woman now, am I? You make me sound like your bit on the side.' She sipped more wine, looking over the rim of her glass.

'My bit on the side, my wife, my best friend, all rolled into one.'

'You always were a smooth talker, James Craig.'

He grinned. 'Has my charm worked on you?'

'I'm tired, honey, sorry,' she said.

'Don't worry, I brought a good book to read.'

She laughed. 'Okay, you talked me into it.'

Finn looked at Craig for a moment as if he knew, but then laid his head back down again.

'Did you know that Clark kept newspaper clippings on the boards on the wall in his study?'

'No. What clippings?'

'Relating to Stuart Hunt's murder. Delphin told me she saw them one day when Clark went down to answer a knock at the front door. He had been in his study and left the door open. She looked in as she walked past.'

'He always kept it locked. I've never been in there.'

'I was in there today. Doing some work on my laptop,' he quickly added. 'There was nothing there. Somebody took all the clippings down.'

'Who would do that?'

Craig looked at her, thinking that maybe he'd put his foot in it. *Why, his killer, my dear.* Instead, he decided to play dumb. 'I have no idea.' Which wasn't a complete lie. He didn't know for sure that somebody had pushed the old man down the stairs. But it was the lollipop in Clark's belongings from the funeral parlour that bothered him. Finding the bag of them in Clark's home could suggest that Clark was the killer they were after, but that night when Craig was sitting in the pouring rain with a lollipop stick being pointed at his eyeball, he'd known that wasn't Clark. Clark would have been fifty-two back then, and he'd been injured on the job years back, badly breaking his ankle, so he always walked with a slight limp after that and couldn't run like the killer had run that night. Plus, Clark had been overweight back then, and had a much bigger build than the killer.

All day, Craig had been thinking about the bag of lollipops. What if Clark had bought them so he could take one out and confront the killer with it? What if he too suspected that the sweetie was a signature left at the crime scene but couldn't prove it? What if it was something he had seen at a crime scene or had seen in a photo of a crime scene? Why hadn't he just bought one lollipop? Who knew? Clark had a membership for Costco over in Edinburgh, so maybe he'd got the bag there.

When Craig thought about the whole idea of a killer leaving a lollipop behind at a murder scene, it sounded ridiculous. A lollipop! Just thinking about it made him feel foolish, but then again, there'd been no mistaking the lollipop stick held a few centimetres from his eyeball. He had thought about that night many times over the years and had concluded that the killer hadn't rammed that stick into Craig's eye because that would have alerted his colleagues to the lollipop thing. But then why hadn't the killer just rammed a knife in?

Craig thought the killer might be throwing down a challenge to him. *You know who I am. Come and find me.*

What if Clark had figured out who the killer was? That would mean that he knew the killer and had him round to the house. Was that likely? Probably, if the killer then pushed Clark down the stairs.

Craig would have to give this more thought. Looking over at his wife, he was glad they'd brought Finn with them as they usually did when they came to Scotland. Nobody would go near Eve when Finn was around, and he knew the big dog would give his own life protecting his family.

His thoughts turned to his father, DI James Craig, and he wished the old man was still around. But he wasn't. He'd died almost six months after DS Stuart Hunt.

But in very different circumstances.

DI James Craig Senior – Craigie to his friends – stood in front of the mirror wondering if he looked acceptable or whether he was giving Quasimodo a run for his money. Aye, if Sheila – his now deceased wife – would have thought it was okay, it would be okay for his date tonight. Fran would have to take him as he was.

He checked his watch, straightened his tie and made sure he had a packet of mints in his jacket pocket. He was hardly ready to hit the town at his age but respectable enough for a couple of beers at the pub in Kelty.

Fran hailed from there, and it was a nice wee boozer. Of course, he'd told them he was a truck driver. Fran was okay, but she wasn't worth getting his bollocks rearranged for. It was her idea to lie to anybody who asked; he had gone along with it, but it went against the grain.

However, it was what it was. Life had been dull since Sheila had passed. Not that it was all skeet shooting and caviar when she was alive, but they'd enjoyed each other's company. The boys were grown up now, and James Junior was a constable. The thought of what happened last Guy Fawkes Night nearly made him want to go back into the bathroom and throw up. The man who had killed Stuart Hunt had almost killed his son, and Craigie would have been gutted. There was a massive manhunt after Stew was murdered and James was attacked, but all to no avail. The bastard had disappeared into thin air.

They were still looking for him, but nothing had been left behind at the crime scene that could point them towards him.

He heard the car horn outside. Fran in her old jalopy. She insisted on driving if he was going to have a pint. *Not that you're a shite driver,* she had told him one night, *but I'd like to get home in one piece, not pieces.*

Fair dos. He liked a pint now and again, and if a woman was willing to drive and drink Coke all night, then who was he to argue?

He rushed downstairs, not wanting to seem too keen but not wanting keep her waiting either.

She smiled and waved from the driver's seat. Fran made him feel good when he saw her. Not as good as he had felt when he saw his Sheila, but it wasn't as if he was going to marry Fran. They were just friends, and not friends with benefits, as his manky son liked to say.

'Come on in, my wee lemon meringue pie,' Fran laughed. She was always jolly, like she had banged her head and was looking at the world through a different set of glasses now, where everybody was nice and nobody got aggravated with each other. Either that or she was on drugs.

'Hello, my wee mince pie,' Craigie said, looking at her.

'Mince pie? Are you suggesting I'm fat and lumpy?'

'Mince pies are no' fat and lumpy,' Craigie said, leaning over to kiss her. Maybe there were a few benefits there, but he wouldn't tell that son of his.

Fran laughed. 'Just winding you up there, Craigie. I'll be anything you want me to be.' She laughed as she pulled away.

And there we have it, Craigie thought. Fran was keen to take their relationship to the next level, but he wasn't quite ready. He didn't know what it was, but the thought of getting undressed in Fran's bedroom – even taking his socks off – shut him down mentally. He should have known she might want to take their relationship to the next level, but it had started with her asking him if she could buy him a drink in the pub one night. He'd been sitting with some of his pals from the station, and he knew they would have ripped the piss out of him, so he said yes, of course she could, and he moved to another table with her, and that was the start of things.

That had been three weeks ago, and she was starting to drop hints about staying over at his house or him at hers, and each time he'd made some flimsy excuse.

He would dump her if she dropped a hint at him tonight. He couldn't sleep with another woman, not yet, not so close to Sheila moving on.

They were heading up towards Kelty on a little back road when Fran noticed the car behind them.

'That joker's flashing his lights,' she said, looking in the rearview mirror. 'I wonder what's wrong?'

Craigie turned round and looked out the back window, seeing the guy flashing his lights. 'Looks like he just wants to pass. It's what a driver behind you does when he wants to pass.' He didn't add that she should have known that since she was an experienced driver; he let it go.

The car roared up behind them, the driver still flashing the lights, and he pulled out to overtake. Then Craigie and Fran heard an almighty bang and felt a violent lurch as the car behind them hit the back of their vehicle.

Fran fought to keep control, but it was no good. Her old saloon spun round, and despite her hitting the brakes, they left the road and crashed down an embankment, tearing through heavy brush until they hit the treeline.

The car smashed into a tree, coming to a dead stop, throwing them both forward. Fran smacked her face on the airbag and was knocked unconscious.

Craigie went through the windscreen.

Fran didn't remember much when she woke up, but now she was in a hospital bed. She hurt, and her face felt like she had been in the ring with Mike Tyson. Machines beeped, telling the nursing staff she was still alive, and some kind of drip was attached to her arm.

A nurse came into the room, saw she was awake and smiled at her. 'Hi, Fran. I'm Julie, one of the nurses here. I'm glad to see you're back with us.'

'What...what happened?' Fran asked.

'I'll have the doctor come and talk to you. But first, there are a couple of men out here waiting to speak with you. They're police officers.'

'Wait...' Fran said, but Julie left, and a few moments later, two men in suits walked in.

'I'm DCI Bill Walker. This is DI Mark Baker.

We'd like to have a word with you about the accident you were in.'

Fran looked puzzled. 'Where's James? James Craig. He was in the car with me.' She saw a flash of a figure going through her windscreen.

'That's what we want to talk to you about. James was pronounced dead at the scene.'

'Oh God, no.' Fran's lip began to tremble. 'I wish I could have outrun him.'

Walker looked at Baker, then back at Fran.

'Outrun who?'

'The guy who smashed into us. He was driving like a maniac, flashing his lights, and then the next thing I knew, he hit my car. I don't remember anything after that.' Tears were running down her face now, and the monitor indicated her heart rate was going up.

'You didn't see anybody? Didn't see the driver?' Baker asked.

She shook her head slowly. 'I'm sorry. It was over in a flash. I remember screaming as we went down the embankment. Then...nothing.'

'We'll be in touch again, Fran,' Walker said. 'Sometimes, things come back to people. We can get a formal statement when you're feeling better. We'll let you rest now.'

ICE INTO ASHES

With that, the two detectives left.

Craig had already handed in his notice to transfer to the Met when Fran called and asked if he would go with her to the impound yard where her car had been taken. The insurance company was still deciding what to do, but she needed to recover her handbag from it.

Craig said he would be happy to go with her. She wanted to go to Craigie's funeral, and Craig said he would be pleased if she were there.

At the impound yard office, Fran was told her handbag was there. They had taken what they could find and put it in a bag for her.

While she was sorting that, Craig walked over to the car, his eyes fixed on the broken windscreen his father had gone through. He walked up to it and peered inside. There was debris inside. Some old fast food wrappers. But the one thing that caught his eye was lying in the passenger footwell.

A lollipop.

Craig felt his heart beating faster as the memories flooded back. His dad had died of blunt force trauma to the head due to the automobile accident and had been buried ten days after the crash. Fran had never been able to give the police any more details about the car or driver who had hit her, and they had never been traced.

Fran had later drowned in a bathtub after drinking a bottle of vodka a year after his dad had died. She had never got over what had happened that night, she told her friends, but they were all surprised she had done something stupid like get drunk and get into a bath.

As far as Craig knew, no lollipops were found in her flat.

But then again, nobody was looking for any.

FIFTEEN

The day started out cold in Dalgety Bay. Ice was on Craig's windscreen, and Eve's too. He looked at his watch and decided he didn't have time to scrape the ice off hers, but he did it anyway.

Ten minutes later, he was done and on his way to Glasgow.

He drove over the Queensferry Crossing and joined the M9, then connected with the M8 and let the car's adaptive cruise control do the driving. His thoughts went to speaking with Dr Callum Strachan, Olivia's father.

Craig had never met the man before but knew of his reputation. He was very well respected in his field, as Olivia had been. Craig's boss, Barry Norman, was Strachan's friend and spoke very highly of him professionally. But what did he know? He couldn't even hit a golf ball into a wee glass five feet away.

Craig took the exit and followed the directions the sat nav was giving him, keeping his fingers crossed that the machine wasn't playing with him and taking him miles away from his destination, like when you stopped for directions and some smartarse sent you in the opposite direction.

His thoughts turned to Clark's study and the newspaper clippings he'd had on his wall. If the old man had suspicions about somebody, why didn't he tell his best friend, Mickey Thompson? Craig made a mental note to talk to Mickey later.

He arrived at the Helen Street police station in Glasgow, a high-security station. At the reception desk, he was told that DCI Angie Fisher would be right down.

He wasn't sure what to expect, but she turned out to be a woman in her mid-forties, he guessed, which would fit with her rank.

'DCI Craig?' she said, smiling and holding out her hand.

'The one and only,' he said, shaking her hand. 'DCI Fisher, I presume? And I don't mean to sound like Sherlock Holmes.'

'That's me.'

'Call me Jim.'

'Angie.'

He looked at her, the blonde hair cut short but not too short. Her eyes were sharp and he guessed she never missed much.

'Thank you for coming with me today. I thought it might be best if a serving police officer from Scotland came with me.'

'No problem. Harry McNeil said you had spoken to him and he suggested me, so when I ran it past my boss, she said that was fine.'

They left the reception and headed into the car park.

'Maybe best if we take my car,' she said. 'Unless you're familiar with Glasgow?'

'Not so much, so I'm happy with your car.'

'How do you like working in London?' she asked as she started the car and they moved out of the car park.

'It's hectic. But it keeps me busy, so I can't complain.'

'My ex-husband worked there. We're getting back together again. He's moved up here but works in another station.'

'Good for you. It's not often that couples get divorced and get back together.'

'We were working up in your area, in Falkland. I can't talk about the case, but it was traumatic, and my ex had family up here. Long story short, we sat and talked, and we're back together.'

'Good for you. I'm glad you have a happy ending.'

'What about you? You married?' Angie asked.

'Twenty-four years next year. We met in high school, and we've been together ever since. She got a teaching job offer in London, and I didn't want to stop her, so I told her to go for it. When she was accepted, I transferred to the Met.'

'You'll notice a big difference to Scotland then?'

'We have eighteen members in our MIT, just one of several. We're kept busy.'

'I bet you are.' Angie started heading west out of the city. 'Callum Strachan is in private practice, so we're heading to his house now. I contacted him, and he said he would be free this morning to talk about his daughter.'

'That's great. I appreciate you doing that.'

'We help each other out, Jim, right?'

'We do that.'

Callum Strachan's house was a detached

bungalow in Bearsden, built in the day when the only tick-tock was the noise from a grandfather clock. It looked like something from the fifties, with attic space turned into a room or rooms, if the skylight was anything to go by.

'Here we are,' Angie said, turning the engine off.

It was still cold outside but damper now, like the snow was waiting to blooter them.

They walked up the wide driveway. There was a garage in the back and a door on the side of the house as well as at the front. Craig looked and wondered if either of them was going to open. Angie was heading for the front door when Craig saw the side door opening and an older man standing there.

'Angie,' Craig said, and she turned to look at him. 'Side door.' He nodded in the direction of Callum Strachan, or at least the man he assumed was Callum.

She walked back towards him and looked around the house at the man and then at Craig. 'I've never met him before, but he fits the description,' she said in a low voice.

'Dr Strachan?' Craig said loudly, like they were there to arrest him for shoplifting or something.

'Aye. Come away in. I've got the kettle on.' Strachan turned away from the door and walked back inside. Craig stepped forward, but Angie beat him to the door.

'Maybe best I go in first since I called him,' she said.

He nodded, about to say, *I can always try and stem the blood flow if he runs you through with a sword*, but he thought that Angie probably wouldn't have been put off by any weapon, Samurai or anything else.

They were confronted by nothing more dangerous than a whistling kettle. Craig guessed the doctor had been nebbing through the net curtains when they pulled up and had hurried through to the kitchen to prepare tea and coffee. Maybe a wee Jammie Dodger thrown in for good measure.

'Make yourselves comfortable!' Strachan shouted through from another room, presumably the kitchen. They had stepped into what looked like a sparsely furnished living room. It made an IKEA display look like an absolute shambles. There were some prints on the walls, one of the sea crashing over a giant rock on the beach somewhere. A watercolour of a girl wearing red walking along a forest trail.

There was a two-seater couch against the back wall, a single chair next to it, and a leather office chair with a small table in front of it. There was a bookshelf with medical books on it, and Craig scanned the titles to see if there was anything of interest, like how to sew your leg back on after drinking and playing with a chainsaw. There was no such title, but there were plenty about the mind, which was to be expected since Strachan was a psychiatrist and not a butcher.

'I see you like my collection of books,' Strachan said, coming in with a tray holding teacups, a teapot with its sweater on, a little jug containing what was probably milk but could have been piss for all Craig knew, and a bowl with a spoon sticking out of it.

Strachan was starting to go red in the cheeks, like he was about to toss the tray onto the carpet, having realised his ambition outweighed his ability when he had picked the tray up. Angie stepped forward and took the tray from him.

'Thank you. I'm not as fit as I used to be.'

'No problem,' she said, looking around for somewhere to put it. Not finding anywhere, she turned to look at Craig for help. Strachan turned away and left the room, and Craig just shrugged his shoulders in a *fucked if I know* way.

Strachan had created a problem and then found the solution by bringing in a small table. 'I keep a nest of tables in the other room,' he said, setting it down in front of the couch. There was a bit of no man's land between that and the office chair, but at least that had the benefit of being on wheels, although how well it travelled over the carpet, Angie didn't know.

Strachan left the room.

Craig didn't want to appear sexist by taking the tray, so he watched Angie walk over to the table, trying not to trip over her feet. Craig pictured this in his mind and knew he would probably laugh if that happened.

'Little help would be good,' she said to him. 'I can't quite see where to land this thing.'

Craig didn't know if she wanted directions or relief from the weight, but he took it and laid it down. 'Teamwork,' he said.

'I need a bloody cup of tea after handling that thing,' Angie said.

'Aye, the tray feels like it was carved from an oak tree.'

Strachan returned with the remaining two tables that made up the nest, one tucked in under the other. 'Handy little buggers, these,' he said, his fingers letting go of the small table in front of the single chair.

'Thanks,' Angie said, plonking herself in the

chair as Strachan put the other table in front of his office chair.

'Milk and one?' he asked Angie. 'Two?'

'Just milk, thanks, Doctor,' she replied. Craig was still standing, and Strachan looked at him, silently asking the same question.

'Same for me, thanks, Doctor.'

'No sugar? However are we going to keep dentists in a job?' Strachan replied, pouring the tea into three cups. 'Please call me Callum. My title is for my patients only. My friends and those I invite over may call me by my given name.'

'Thanks, Callum,' Angie said.

'Cheers,' Craig said, not wanting to be too pally with the old doctor, especially since he hadn't bothered to put any biscuits out. Not even rich teas, which were usually only reserved for filling holes in plasterboard. Craig didn't take sugar in his tea, but he wasn't opposed to creating some cavities with the odd biscuit. Still, his waistline could do with a rest anyway.

Strachan bustled about and finally sat on his leather chair, looking at each of them in turn as if trying to guess which was mental, before deciding they both were.

'You wanted to talk to me about my daughter,' he

said when neither of them threw out the opening gambit.

'Yes, we did,' Angie said.

Craig sipped his tea without blowing on the surface, an action he immediately regretted. *Oh, ya bastard,* he said to himself, licking his burning lip. Maybe the old boy couldn't spare too much milk, or the tea was meant to sit for a while, but either way, it hurt like a bitch.

'Could you tell me a little about Olivia's background?' Craig said, putting his cup down on the table.

'Olivia has a brilliant mind,' Strachan began, and Craig noticed he hadn't touched his tea. 'She's a brilliant psychiatrist, far better than I am. Maybe it's the maternal instinct in her combined with the training, but she was perfect when she was practising. Then it all happened. With that animal.'

'Bruce King,' Craig said.

Strachan looked at him, and there was a slight change in his demeanour, like he was mentally reaching for a gun. 'Yes. That bastard. The damage he did.'

'Olivia seems to be coping better each time I see her. And now she's going for short walks accompanied.'

'Is the person who goes with her able to defend her? Are they a black belt in kung fu or something? Olivia would curl up into a ball if King approached her in the street and said boo to her.'

'I'll call Harry McNeil again, see if he can have one of his officers go with her. I can go too, but two of us with her would be good protection for her.'

'Thank you.'

'I could always go through to Edinburgh too,' Angie said.

'That's very kind, both of you,' Strachan said.

Craig decided to go with the tea again, blowing over the surface this time before taking a sip. Still too hot. He put the cup down. 'I wanted to ask you about something,' he said to Strachan.

'Oh yes? Fire away.'

'Have you received a photo in the post recently?' Craig expected the older man to ask, *A photo of what?* But he merely stood up and left the room.

'Was it something I said?' Craig asked.

Angie shrugged her shoulders. 'It seemed like a reasonable question to me.'

Strachan returned a few moments later holding an envelope. He passed it to Craig. 'Like this one?' he said, sitting back down again.

Craig took out a pair of nitrile gloves, Angie did

the same, and it was almost as if they were racing to see who could snap them on first. Angie won. Craig was hindered by his giant fingers, which had come in handy when he had been cornered once and had to come out fighting, his fingers curled into fists. When the gloves were on, he looked at the front of the envelope. The postmark was from Edinburgh.

He opened it, and inside was a photo, a normal six-by-four. He took it out and looked at it. The picture was of a hammer, a simple claw one with a rubber handle. It looked like the kind that was sold in any DIY shop. He turned the photo over and saw the writing on it.

Your daughter will work this one out before you do. She's the superior out of the two of you, after all. We've met before. We'll meet again.

'When did this arrive?' Angie asked after Craig handed the photo over to her.

'A few days ago.'

'Is this the first time you've had something like this?'

Strachan nodded. 'Yes. I don't know who this person is or why he's sending me a photo like this. Maybe he's trying to intimidate me for some reason. I did think it was Bruce King, playing games with us, but now I'm not so sure.'

'Maybe another former patient?' Angie said, putting the photo back in the envelope and handing it back to Craig.

'I've had a few over the years, right enough, but I can't think of any particular one who would do this sort of thing. Besides, they weren't psychopathic.'

'Do you mind if I keep this?' Craig asked. 'I'd like to have it analysed.'

'Fine by me.'

'Not that I think they'll find anything useful on it,' Craig added, 'but you never know.'

'I think somebody's trying to scare Olivia and put the wind up me as well.'

'Just be on your guard,' Angie said. 'Here's my business card. Call me any time.'

'Thank you.'

'Maybe one day Olivia will be able to get back out and feel safe,' Craig said, 'and come back home here to be with you.'

'Did she live at home with you here?' Angie asked.

Strachan shook his head. 'No. I moved to Glasgow after Olivia was attacked. We lived in your part of the world, DCI Craig. Dunfermline. That's where Olivia was born and brought up.'

'Really?' Craig said. 'I didn't realise.'

Strachan nodded. 'Oh yes, Olivia was drawn by the big city lights of Edinburgh. She always loved going over there when she was a child. It was a treat for her, and the allure was always there.'

'Were you still in Dunfermline when she was attacked?'

'I was. I told her she should have stayed over in the Kingdom, but what do I know?' Strachan sounded bitter, frustrated and angry. 'She might never have met that mutant.'

'Have you ever heard from Bruce King?' Angie said.

'No.'

'Olivia told me one of the times I was up here that she couldn't even be certain her attacker was King. She was ninety per cent sure it was him, but not a hundred per cent. What are your thoughts on that?' Craig asked.

Strachan breathed in through his nose and out his mouth as if he was preparing to answer a halfwit. 'She saw the watch he was wearing. It was a fake gold Rolex. He had told her about it one day, said that somebody had bought it for him in a shop in Singapore or something. She didn't see her attacker's face, but she saw the watch.'

'Did he say anything to her when he was attacking her?' Angie asked.

Strachan shook his head. 'Not that she told me.'

'Was her mother around when Olivia was attacked?' Angie said.

Strachan was silent for a moment as if gathering his thoughts. 'No. She had been dead a year. It hit Olivia hard. Harder than it hit me. I was devastated, but she and Olivia had a special bond. To lose my wife was one thing, but to lose my daughter a year later was devastating.' He looked at the two detectives. 'I know she's alive, but she's in that place, and I might as well have lost her.'

'How do you feel about her going out and about now?'

'I would encourage it. I think if King was going to get in touch with her, then he would have done so already, don't you?'

Craig didn't mention the writing on the photo sent to Olivia. 'Maybe you're right, Doctor. It's been a long time, after all.'

Strachan smiled, but it was strained.

'We'll get going now. Thank you for meeting with us.'

'Any time.'

Craig and Angie stood up, and Strachan saw them out.

'Don't ever take your safety for granted,' Craig said to him at the door.

'Trust me, I never do,' Strachan said.

The air felt cold in the car, but Angie's heated seats promised heat and comfort in a few minutes.

'What do you think of him?' Angie asked as she drove away.

'I think he's an angry father,' Craig said. 'And I don't blame him.'

'He seems sure that Bruce King won't be coming back.'

'Seems reasonable enough. I mean, I think King would have got fed up waiting around for years to try and attack Olivia again. People like him tend to move on to another, easier target.'

'True.'

They got back to Helen Street, where Angie parked close to Craig's car.

'The offer still stands for me to come through and join you on the walkabout with Olivia,' she said to him.

'What about your boss? Won't she have something to say about that?'

'Lynn McKenzie is one of the best. I'm sure she'll

be fine when I tell her it's all part of an ongoing investigation. We're still looking for this guy, aren't we?'

'The case is still open, but calling it active is a little stretch.'

'Don't tell me: if any other evidence comes up, we'll look into it.'

'You can tell your boss that both Olivia and her father have been sent photos apparently from a serial killer working on my patch in London.'

'I will. But I wonder, why now? I mean, you're up here for a funeral, and suddenly, your man sends a photo to a woman you know up here and her father. Something's not right.'

'I know what you mean. Something's not sitting well with me about that. How did he get Callum Strachan's address?'

'Do you think Bruce King is *The Hammer*?' Angie asked.

'It's one avenue to explore. Never say never, eh?' He smiled at her, shrugging his overcoat up further, battling the cold after they got out of the car.

'Let me give you a call about going to see Olivia.'

'I think she wants to go tomorrow.'

'I'll be there, Jim.'

'What about plans with your ex? Or not your ex anymore?'

'Dougie will be just fine.'

'Great. I'll call Olivia to double-check she still wants to go, and then I can call you instead of you calling me.'

'Sounds like a plan.'

Craig got back into his car and headed back home.

SIXTEEN

Craig found a radio station playing eighties tunes. The best decade for music, his father had said. He was into retro music, and somehow Craig Junior had caught the bug. 'Life in a Northern Town' by The Dream Academy was playing. He thought that applied to him in a way, except the town he was driving over to was quite a bit further north than the town in the song.

The sky was like a colour photo that had been Photoshopped to make it look like a black-and-white one, and the day had turned out to be dank and dreary. People were driving around, going to work and coming back from work, their day filled with work-related projects. He couldn't envision anybody driving about for enjoyment.

The Edinburgh Christmas market was on, though, so that could be a draw for some. Then Craig had an idea: what if he and Angie took Olivia to the market? Would she be able to handle the crowds? He believed that Bruce King was long gone and they had to convince Olivia of that. To open the door to a brighter future than being shut in the hospital. He would run it by her and see.

When he got home, Eve was out, but Finn was pleased to see him as usual. The dog rubbed himself against him, waiting to be petted. Craig obliged.

After he managed to dislodge himself from the dog's attention, he let him out into the back garden, where the dog peed and then came right back in. Finn looked at him as if to say, *So I'm not getting a walk, lazy bastard?*

'Later, boy. I promise.' The dog ran away and came back with a rubber ball and dropped it at Craig's feet. Back home, a dog walker came every weekday to play with the dog and exercise him, and Craig didn't know how the young woman could do this every day. It was different when it was for money, he thought.

After tossing the ball – avoiding photo frames sitting on a small table, the prints on the wall and a lamp at the side of a chair – it was time to sit down and count himself lucky that he hadn't managed to tan a window.

He thought about Clark again, convinced now that the old man was murdered. It was the lollipops, and even though just thinking about the sweeties made Craig question his theory, if not quite his sanity, he was convinced that the killer had left them at crime scenes throughout the years. Usually, a killer left a signature in order to be recognised, but this killer left them for his satisfaction.

Craig knew it would be impossible to go through records of...what? Old men who had fallen down the stairs? No, this killer was much more intelligent than that. His MO wasn't just to kill old men.

His thoughts were interrupted by his phone ringing. It was his boss, DSup Barry Norman.

'Hey, boss,' he said.

'Jimmy, I have some news. The bastard struck again. A woman in her twenties, walking her dog.'

'Oh Christ. Where was she killed?'

'In a park. No witnesses. A dog walker found her dead, the dog going mental. He killed the woman, and he left the hammer by her side. Same one that he sent me a photo of. She's been dead for days.'

'God Almighty.' Craig looked at Finn and hoped that nobody would ever touch his son. That would reveal a side of him that nobody had ever seen. 'Any relatives?' he asked.

'She was married. We just tracked him down, and he's been told. He's a wreck. So either a great actor or not our killer.'

'I visited Olivia Strachan yesterday. Our killer sent her a photo I've just returned from visiting her father in Glasgow with a detective from over there, and he was also sent a photo. I'll have somebody send them to the lab, but I doubt there'll be any DNA or prints on them.'

'What? How the hell did that happen? I mean, how does he know your connection to them both?'

'I have no idea. But Olivia thinks it's somebody close to me or who at least knows me, and I tend to agree with her.'

There was silence for a moment.

'Or it could be me, Jimmy. I'm friends with Strachan. Maybe somebody knows about me and is taunting me. He did send me a photo of the murder weapon, after all.'

'Could be.' *Or it could be that he's clever and trying to throw us off the scent.*

'Be careful, Jimmy. Just watch your back up there.'

'I will, sir.'

'Good man. Stay in touch. Let me know how the funeral goes.'

'I will.'

Craig hung up and dialled his son's number, not expecting him to answer, but he did.

'Joe, it's Dad.'

'Hi, Dad,' a female voice said.

'Who's this?' Craig asked, adrenaline kicking in.

The female laughed, and he heard her talking away from the phone and another voice chiming in.

'Hi, Dad, sorry about that.'

'Who is that, Joe?' Craig asked, unable to keep the irritation out of his voice.

'It's my girlfriend.'

There was silence for a few moments.

'You didn't tell us you were dating.'

'I *have* been out with other women, Dad. I don't make a report every time I go out with one.'

Craig heard the female laughing in the background. *Cheeky cow.* 'I know that, son. Anyway, I was calling to see if you fancy a pint tonight?'

'Tonight? Oh man, I'm busy. Maybe some other time?'

'I'm only up here with your mum for the funeral, Joe.'

'I know that, and I'm going to be there too,

remember?'

'Okay, that's fine. But I'd still like to see you before I go south.'

'I'll see you, Dad, don't worry.'

Craig heard the laughter in the background. This was one girlfriend he didn't like, and he hadn't even met the lassie.

'Okay, give me a call when you have a spare minute. Take care, son.'

'I will, Dad. Later.'

The call was ended, and Craig sat for a minute, shaking his head. He called Eve. It was late afternoon, and he didn't know where she was. 'Hi, honey. I'm back at the house now. I was wondering what you fancied doing for dinner.'

'To be honest, I was at the solicitor's this afternoon, and I bumped into Rose. She had a day off, so we went for a late lunch. I'm not that hungry. Can you fix something for yourself?'

'No problem. I have to swing by the station to drop some things off for the lab. I'll grab something when I'm out. I'll feed the boy before I go.'

'Just don't leave him on his own too long. You know he needs to go out not long after eating.'

'Maybe I should delay his dinner. It is a bit early, right enough. He won't starve.'

'That's fine.'

'Talking of the boy, I called the other one. Did you know he's got a new girlfriend?'

'They're always going out with girls. You know what students are like.'

'He used the word "girlfriend," not a girl who's a friend.'

There was silence on the other end for a moment before Eve answered. 'I had a coffee with him when I first arrived. I drove up to St Andrews, and he didn't say a word. I wonder why he mentioned it to you and not me?'

'He didn't have a choice; she answered his phone. From what I could hear in the background, she thought it was funny, all giggling and laughing.'

'She sounds like a charmer. I can't wait to meet her.'

'He couldn't make it for a pint tonight, so I told him I'd see him at the funeral.'

'Couldn't make it for a pint with his dad when he doesn't get to see you that often? Christ, what happened to him, Jim? He always wanted to go for a pint when you came up.'

'He's twenty-one and growing up fast; that's what happened.'

'I'd like to see him socially before we return to

London,' Eve said.

'I'm sure we will.'

'Call me later. I won't be that long.'

'Just take care, Eve.'

'I always do.'

'Love you.'

'Love you too.'

He hung up and felt a steel ball dropping into his stomach. Joe was his only child, and he would do anything for his son, and he didn't like the fact that he was seeing some cheeky wee bint.

He got up and let the dog out the back again, and Finn peed. If history were anything to go by, the grass would have yellow dead spots on it by summer.

'Dad won't be long, pal.'

Finn tilted his head sideways, trying to translate what his human was saying. Food? Play? Jump on the furniture when you're gone?

Craig went through to the kitchen, Finn on bodyguard duty, and he gave the dog a treat from a bag Eve had bought.

'Be good. If you're going to eat slippers, make sure they're Mummy's.' He patted the dog on the head and put his jacket on.

Downstairs, he realised he hadn't stuck his head into Clark's garage. The old man had told Craig the last time he'd seen him that he was planning to buy another car.

He opened the door and saw the old, familiar Renault sitting there. Clark hadn't got around to trading it in. There was nothing wrong with the old car, but he had been a man who only kept a car for a little while.

Craig stepped into the garage and had a look around. After the funeral, he and Eve would have to go through the stuff and arrange for a company to come in and haul the junk away.

He looked at the shelves on one side of the double garage. It had one large door and was big enough to fit two cars, but Hilda hadn't driven in years, so they'd kept one car and used the other half for storage.

Craig felt like a housebreaker as he scanned the boxes. It was like peeking behind the door of somebody else's life, going through their stuff while they were out. He felt sad as he realised that Clark was never coming back.

There were plastic boxes stacked on shelves opposite the car, clear ones with stuff packed into them that Clark and Hilda had presumably collected over the years. Maybe it was belongings they had brought from the old house and never sorted out.

Craig saw a box that held toy cars. He took it off the shelf and took the lid off, looking inside. There were Matchbox cars still in their boxes. Little police cars and vans made by Oxford Diecast. He wondered why Clark hadn't found shelf space for them.

He put the lid back on and put the box back on the shelf. There were other boxes with books in them: paperbacks, some with the charity shop sticker still on the front.

He turned towards the garage door and saw the recycling and rubbish bins. He wasn't sure when they had to be put outside, and he was curious to see if there was anything in them. He didn't want anything going rotten and smelling up the place.

He lifted the lid of the rubbish bin and saw there was nothing inside. Then, the recycling bin.

There were papers in it. Craig looked closer and saw they were newspaper clippings, scrunched up and tossed in the bin. Then he realised what he was looking at: the clippings Delphin said she saw on Clark's study wall.

Whoever took them down had dumped them in here.

Clark's killer.

SEVENTEEN

Craig drove through the rain up the A82, having called Isla McGregor before he left the house. He had put on gloves and taken the papers out and put them into a bin liner, then deposited them in the study.

He would need to sit down with Eve and tell her his thoughts and be prepared for her to laugh at him. He was glad Isla hadn't laughed at him when he'd had her around at the house. She still might if he told her about the lollipop theory.

It wasn't the woman in reception this time but some grumpy old bastard who looked like he'd sat on a poker and it was still up his arse.

'Help you?' he said in a tone that said, *This better be good.*

'DCI James Craig, here to see DS Isla McGregor.'

'Who?'

'Me or Isla?' Craig wasn't sure who the man was confused over.

The man curled his lip. He looked to be around sixty, riding out his shifts until retirement, and thinking this tosser who had just walked in off the street was impersonating a copper.

'It's okay, Tam,' Isla said, poking her head into the reception area from the staff corridor.

'What's okay?' Tam said.

'Belligerent *and* fucking daft,' Craig said to himself.

Tam turned to him. 'Daft but not deaf. You can take that fake warrant card and shove it up your arse.'

'Tam, it's fine. Let him in. He's working on a case with me.'

Tam curled his lip and shuffled away after pressing the button to unlock the door, probably wishing it was a detonator button.

'Nice meeting you, Tam,' Craig said, walking past the doorway, trying to soften the blow he'd been dealt.

'Sod off.'

Isla laughed as they walked along towards the

lifts. 'He's been a fixture around here for a long time. Retirement's calling his name, and he's counting the days. He used to work in Dunfermline, but for some reason, he got shifted up here.'

'I wonder why,' Craig said, shaking his head. 'I have the photos here,' he went on, reaching into his pocket. 'There's three of them, each in its own envelope.' He held out the three envelopes for her to see as if he was waiting for her to choose one to see if she'd won a holiday or a coffee colonic irrigation.

She took all three. 'I'll have them taken along to Dundee later on today,' she said.

He realised she must have thought he was a plank, coming upstairs with her when he could have just given her the envelopes in the corridor downstairs. Maybe he subconsciously figured he would sit her down now and tell her the theory he'd had for years. It wasn't just a theory, he reminded himself. The bastard had held a lollipop stick to his eyeball, which at the very least would have ruptured his eye, putting an end to his career.

'Would you have time for a coffee?' he asked her.

She smiled and nodded. 'Of course.'

They got out of the lift and walked along to the canteen. It was winding down for the day, so it wasn't busy. DS Dan Stevenson was at one of the vending machines. He looked around when he saw Isla and Craig approach the counter.

'How do, boss?' Stevenson said.

'Not so bad,' Craig answered. 'Just here on a bit of business,' he added, in case Stevenson thought he was here to have it away with the young female sergeant.

'None of my business what you do in your own time.' Stevenson smiled at his quip and returned to looking at the treasure trove of bad cholesterol and high blood sugar behind the protective glass.

Craig and Isla stood in line for the coffees, and they sat at a table away from the other uniforms and personnel.

'I'll get the envelopes over to the lab as soon as possible, but they might not be able to get to them until Monday. Even if they will accept them tonight.'

'Monday's fine. There's probably nothing on them that we can use, forensically speaking, but I'd like them checked over. I'm hunting a serial killer in London, and now he's sent three photos of a hammer to people in Scotland, two of whom I know, the third related to one of the others.'

'I don't think there'll be anything on them, but we have to try, right?' Isla said.

'Right.' Craig looked round at the sound of

thumping on glass. It was Dan with a fist on the machine.

'You okay there, big man?' he asked.

Dan turned to look at him. 'Bastard machine ate my coins. Imagine that, getting robbed in a police station. There's no sanctuary, is there?'

Craig laughed. 'Grab yourself a coffee and join us.' He reached into his pocket, took out a coin, and flipped it to Dan, who caught it like he had practised this trick at home.

'Still the last of the big spenders, Jimmy boy, I see,' he said, laughing.

'Jimmy boy?' Isla said in a low voice. 'That's stepping over the line a bit, right?'

Craig shook his head. 'Dan and I go way back. He saved my life when I was in uniform. I moved to London shortly afterward, and we didn't keep in touch, which was all my fault. Even when I came here to visit, I didn't connect with Dan. I want to make up for it now.'

'By buying him a cup of coffee?'

'Yeah, that.'

'Respect where respect is due. You're still a DCI.'

'Not up here I'm not.' Craig turned to look at the big man standing at the counter. 'I never let a day go by that I'm not thankful for that man. A serial killer was about to end my life when Big Dan came running at him like a train, shouting. If he hadn't, I'd be dead, no doubt about it.'

Isla looked over at Dan, a newfound respect for him showing. 'I didn't know that about him.'

'I don't suppose he shouts about it.'

Then Dan was over at their table. He was still a big man, but none of it was fat. He looked like he looked after himself at the gym. His short hair was greyer now, but then so was Craig's.

'How's life treating you?' Craig asked him.

'Not too bad, Jimmy,' Dan said, putting his lips to the mug like he was about to taste cat piss for the first time. He took a sip and then nodded. 'I'm pleasantly surprised; it doesn't taste like it was gobbed in.'

Craig looked down at his coffee. 'I didn't know that was a thing, or I would have paid extra to have it left out.'

'There was a boy off sick, and he swears it was because of something he ate here. I don't believe it; he's a fat pig who stops at Tim Hortons on the way home.' Dan took another sip. 'How's things with you?'

'I'm up from London for Clark Brown's funeral. He was my wife's uncle.'

'Oh aye, I heard about that. The old boy fell down the stairs or something. Poor sod.'

'He did.' Craig quickly looked at Isla, who didn't let on that she had been at the house, helping to test out Craig's theory about how Clark could have been murdered.

'You married Eve, didn't you?' Dan asked.

'I did. She got the job in London, so I transferred.'

'Aye, I remember that. Thanks for the wedding invite, by the way.'

'Back at you.'

Dan grinned. 'You were down south when Linda and I got hitched. Coming up for our twenty-fifth soon.'

'Kids?'

'Aye. Two daughters. Apple of their daddy's eye, and they wrap me around their little finger.'

'Glad to hear that, Dan.' Craig looked at his colleague, who must be around fifty now, three years older than Craig himself, and he wondered why he wasn't in charge of MIT by now.

'What about you? Any heirs?'

'One. Joe. He's a student in St Andrews.'

'St Andrews Uni? Nice.'

'Eve's parents left her money in their will for

Joe's education, and he wanted to return to Scotland.'

'Going to be polis like his dad, do you think?'

'God knows what he's going to do. He's studying IT or something.'

'Or something?' Isla said. 'What's the *or something*?'

'No idea.' Craig sipped his coffee, wondering what his son was studying. 'How do you like Bill Walker?' he asked, changing the subject.

'Billy's a good bloke, eh, Isla?'

'He is,' Isla confirmed.

'What about Mark Baker?'

Dan sipped more coffee. 'Mark's more of a politician than anything else. The high heid yins along at the castle shout, and he jumps after it's trickled down to him. Good copper but a bit straight-laced.'

The castle was Tulliallan, the police training college.

'Aye, but he's not afraid to roll up his sleeves, I'll give him that,' Isla confirmed. 'He's always got your back if you're in a sticky wicket. He looks after his team.'

'When's the funeral?' Dan asked Craig.

'Next Monday.'

'You're here for a wee while then?'

'Aye. At least for another week. Eve has to sort out her uncle's affairs.'

'Listen, you fancy grabbing a pint tonight?'

'Sure. That would be great.'

'Where are you staying?' Dan asked.

'We always stayed with Clark in Dalgety Bay, so we figured the old boy wouldn't have minded if we stayed there again.'

'I'm sure he would have thought that's just barry. I'm along in Inverkeithing. I know a good wee boozer in Dunfermline. It's called Pitreavie Golf Club.'

'I live in Dunfermline,' Isla said, smiling.

'That's great, Isla, I'm pleased for you,' Dan said.

'I'm not a golfer,' Craig said.

'Neither am I. I'm just a social member.'

'Great. How about seven?'

'I'm free tonight. Footloose and fiancé-free,' Isla said, grinning.

'Are you really that desperate for male company that you'll hang out with a couple of old geezers?' Dan said.

'Less of the old, Dan,' Craig said.

'A couple of geezers,' Dan said.

'Yes. I have a male cat, but he doesn't count.' She looked at both men in turn. 'Come on, don't make me beg. I haven't been on a night out in ages, and–'

'Fine by me,' Craig said. 'But how am I going to tell my wife I'm going out drinking with another woman?'

'I'm sure you'll think of something. Dan? Would it be alright with your wife if you had a pint with a *colleague*? I mean, it's not as if we haven't had a pint together before –'

'Jesus, Isla. Is this how you wear men down?' Dan said.

She grinned. 'Of course.'

'Seven o'clock at Pitreavie Golf Club,' Dan answered her, finishing his coffee.

'Great. I'll see you both there,' she said, smiling as she picked up the envelopes, and she left the two men alone.

'She's enthusiastic, I'll give her that,' Craig said.

'She doesn't go out much since her boyfriend dumped her for somebody else. Trust issues. My wife won't be bothered if she tags along. Besides, who'd want to go out with an ugly old bastard like me now?'

'That's true.'

'That's the thanks I get after saving your life?' Dan said.

'After twenty-five years, you still won't let me forget, will you?'

'Absolutely not.'

Craig grinned. He'd always liked Dan, even though he'd seemed a bit gruff and jaded when they were both in uniform, after only five years in the force.

'Those envelopes that Isla took?' he said to Dan.

'What about them?'

'Each one has a photo of a hammer. They were sent to Clark, to a woman I know and to her father. The same MO as a serial killer we're trying to find in London, one who's been operating for five years.'

'Jesus.'

'We're no nearer to catching him, and he sent my boss a photo before I left. And he's just struck again, killing a young woman in a park in north London.'

'Why did he send a photo to those other people?'

'It's a personal dig at me. He wants me to know he knows things about me. The bastard.'

'Do you think he knows you're up here in Scotland?'

'Either that or he knows I've been going to see Olivia Strachan in the Royal Ed.'

'You're going to have to give me the rundown on those people.'

'I will. Tonight.'

There was a silence between the two men at that

point. Craig looked at his colleague. 'What's on your mind, Dan?'

Dan took a breath and let it out. 'Nothing, really.'

'It's either nothing or something.'

Dan looked Craig in the eye. 'It's something. When it's in my head, it all seems plausible; people take me seriously, and something's done about it. Then, when I think about telling somebody about my theory, it all goes out the window.'

'I met you a long time ago, and you saved my life. I have no doubt about that. That night, when the killer was leaning over me, about to kill me, you shouted and distracted him, then he took off. If you hadn't turned up, I'd be dead now. Anything you say or want to tell me, I'll listen. Without judgement.' Craig sipped his coffee, which was rapidly going cold.

Dan blew out a breath, not in Craig's direction. 'That night, you were sitting down with your back against the wall of the house. He'd clobbered you, and I don't think I'd ever run as fast as that in my life. My torch was bobbing about, the light bouncing everywhere, and I thought for a minute that the guy wasn't going to move, but then he patted you on the face and took off running into the woods.'

'I know all that, Dan.'

'You wrote in your report that he was holding a knife to your eyeball. But it looked like something else.'

Craig was silent for a moment. 'Like what?' he asked eventually.

Dan hesitated before answering. 'A lollipop stick.'

'A lollipop stick?' Craig said, acting surprised.

'I know it sounds stupid. I told myself I was mistaken, that he was holding a knife up to your face. The ambulance crew arrived, and they took you away, and there were people everywhere. I was about to walk away when I saw it: a lollipop with the wrapper still on it, lying just a few feet away from where you'd been sitting. I ignored it, but up until this day, I've wondered if you were confused and just thought he had a knife at your face.'

Craig maintained eye contact with Dan. 'You weren't mistaken. I thought I'd imagined it, convinced myself I'd imagined it, but the thought has kept returning to me for years. It sounds so bloody stupid when I say it out loud. I sound like I'm daft, but he didn't have a knife that night. He was about to ram a lollipop stick into my eyeball.'

EIGHTEEN

Eve and Rose ended up in Starbucks on North Street across from the Kingdom Shopping Centre in Glenrothes. They sat at a little table, Eve with a hot chocolate and Rose with another Americano.

'This is fun, Eve,' Rose said, sipping her drink. Some schoolkids were coming in now, excited and boisterous, pretending to be adults, drinking coffee and talking like they were ready to take on the world.

'It is. I'm enjoying myself.'

'There are old women out there just waiting to be mugged, post offices to be robbed and drugs to be taken,' Rose said.

'That sounds very cynical for a teacher,' Eve said.

'I'm just going by some of the parents. Honestly,

they drive me insane at times. I've been threatened on more than one occasion.'

'It's the whole British justice system; there are those who think they're better than everybody else, and they're the ones who are going around being protected by men with guns. Jimmy sees it all the time.'

'I'm thinking of getting out of the game now. Find something else to do before I give myself a heart attack.'

Eve smiled. 'You're too old to change careers now. What about your pension?'

'Too old, Eve? Speak for yourself. You might want to look in the fucking mirror sometime.' Rose stood up, grabbed her handbag and headed for the toilets.

Eve was dumbfounded for a moment but knew her friend was under a lot of stress. Her husband leaving her had kicked her hard. She took her phone out and sent a text to her husband, a little emoji. A smiley face with red hearts for eyes. She did think herself lucky to have Jimmy in her life. She would never do anything to destroy what they had; she loved him so much.

Then she fired off a text to her son: *Girlfriend,*

Joe? I don't remember you mentioning her. Tell your mother all about her.

She waited for a reply, but nothing came back. Maybe he was studying. No, there weren't any exams coming up. Studying a female form, more like.

She looked up when she heard shouting and saw Rose standing in front of a woman who looked a bit younger than her, yelling and pointing her finger at the woman.

'You've got a cheek showing your face round here!' Rose shouted, her eyes wide and spittle flying out of her mouth.

'I live here!' the woman screamed back. 'Mind your own business. I hope you're happy with that fucking tosser of a husband of yours.'

Rose looked puzzled. 'What are you slavering about?'

'Oh, look at her!' The woman turned round for effect as if they were on a stage with an audience hanging on to their every word. 'Acting all indignant because her husband left her for me.' She turned to look at Rose again. 'I hope you're both very happy together!'

'What on God's earth are you talking about, woman? He's not with me. You took him, remember?'

The woman went quiet for a moment. 'He left me to go back to you.' Her voice was softer now.

'If he did, then he never came back to me.'

'He sent me a text saying he had made a mistake and was returning to you.'

'That's news to me,' Rose said. Her voice was also lower. 'I divorced him in his absence. I never saw him again after he left me, although he was supposed to come round and sort some stuff out. He never showed up.'

The younger woman shook her head. 'Maybe he left both of us.' She looked Rose in the eye. 'Sorry for shouting.'

'Likewise.'

They parted ways, and Rose came back to the table. 'Thanks for the coffee. I have to go. I'll call you.'

She grabbed her jacket from the back of the chair and walked out.

Eva sat there, shocked, for a moment. What had just gone on? Had Rose's ex played both his wife *and* his girlfriend? Why would he do that?

Her phone dinged. Joe, her son. *I'll have a coffee with you and tell you about her sometime.*

Try to have a pint with your dad. He misses you. Preferably tonight. She wanted to write, *if you can haul yourself away from the floozy*, but kept that bit to herself.

I'll text him and see if he can have a pint tonight, then.

Thank you, Joe. xx

Jim would be pleased, Eve thought, putting her phone away.

She picked up her phone and sent a text to Craig. *Heading home. I have a surprise for you.*

She waited for a response, and it came a few seconds later. *I'm a bit tired, to be honest. It's sort of like jet lag. Car lag.*

She smiled to herself. *For dinner. And you and me both. xx*

He sent her a smiley emoji back, and she got up. Outside, darkness wasn't far away, and the sky was the colour of cement.

She walked over to her Volvo and saw a woman in the car next to hers with her head in her hands on the steering wheel. Then she threw her head back, and Eve could see it was the woman from Starbucks.

Eve knocked on the driver's window. The woman was startled and jumped, not knowing who she was. She wound the window down an inch.

'Yes?'

'Are you okay?' Eve asked.

The woman nodded at first, then changed her mind. 'No. Thanks for asking, though.'

'I'm a friend of Rose's,' Eve said gently. 'I saw what happened in there. I'm sorry you had to go through that.'

'I feel awful about what happened back then. I was stupid to go with a married man.'

'I'm Eve. What's your name?'

'Maggie Marsh.'

'Well, Maggie, what's done is done. We can't change the past.'

'Did you know Henry?' Maggie asked.

Eve nodded. 'I did. We didn't socialise much, though.' She paused. 'How long were you with him before he left?'

'Six months. He told me it was over with Rose. There was nothing there anymore. The thing is, we were happy together. We were going to move south to Manchester. He had family there, he said. Everything was moving along nicely, then suddenly, I got a text from him saying he was going back to his wife and not to contact him again. He sent some abusive texts, telling me I'd split them up and what a bitch I was for doing that. All sorts of stuff. I was glad then that I hadn't moved with him. And now I find out it was all a lie. How stupid am I?'

'Don't blame yourself. These things happen all the time. I know it hurts when it happens to you, but you're better off now.'

'Am I?' Maggie said. 'I'm alone, I can't seem to attract the right sort of man and I'm not getting any younger.' She rolled up her window, started her car and drove away.

NINETEEN

When Craig got home, Eve was frying a couple of steaks on the cooker.

'Hey, honey. How was your day?'

'It was good.'

Finn rubbed himself against his dad's leg, and Craig petted him. 'Who's Dad's boy?'

After what felt like a mild workout rubbing the dog's back and ears, Craig looked at his wife. 'I bumped into Dan Stevenson. We're going for a pint at the Pitreavie Golf Club tonight. Also, full disclosure: DS Isla McGregor is coming along. We're going to discuss some work stuff.'

Eve turned round and smiled. 'Is she young?'

'Yes.'

'Is she pretty?'

'Not as pretty as you.'

'Do I have to be worried?'

'Not any more than usual.'

She laughed. 'That's alright then.'

'Look, I can't help having the looks of a movie star and the body of a gym junkie.'

'Definitely not worried.'

'I feel I'm being mocked here.' He walked over and kissed her.

'The looks of a movie star. Who? Bela Lugosi?'

'You're too young to remember him.'

'I've seen him in old films before.'

Craig shook his head. 'I'm never opening up to you again.'

'Dinner in ten if you want to freshen up.'

'Aye, aye, captain.'

He used the bathroom and then looked at himself in the mirror. He reminded himself to tell Dan about the newspaper clippings. Should he bring Isla into this? *You already did when you invited her round to the house and did a mock-up of a crime scene, remember?*

'Dinner!' Eve shouted.

Craig looked at the clippings. One caught his eye: the death of Stuart Hunt and the manhunt it had sparked as they tried to track down the killer.

The press had spoken to Mark Baker, a DI back then. Baker had told the media that they would stop at nothing to bring the killer to justice.

But of course, they never had.

He left the room and went to the dining room, where Eve had put out two plates, each with a fantastic steak.

'I don't think I could ever be a vegetarian,' Craig said. 'God bless them.'

'Me neither. I like meat too much.' There was a twinkle in her eyes when she said that.

'You're the mother of my child. I don't expect such filth to come out of your mouth.'

She laughed as they sat down.

'Which reminds me, did our heir call you?'

'No. Why?'

'I told the wee bugger to get in touch and have a pint with you.'

Craig had cut off a piece of steak and he held it halfway to his mouth. 'No, you didn't.'

'I bloody well did. He isn't too busy, so he can have a drink with you. You're not asking him to go to a strip club with you or go clubbing all night. A couple of pints won't kill him.'

'You want me to interrogate him about this new girl he has in his life, don't you?'

'If the subject comes up.'

Craig put the steak in his mouth and chewed. He liked his so well done, the fire brigade was on standby. Eve wanted hers so rare, all the butcher had to do was take the horns off and wipe its arse. Opposite ends of the steak-eating scale.

'I have no doubt it will. I'll make sure of it.'

'Good.'

'I'll also make sure that he knows it was your idea.'

'Please do. You know he won't call me and give me any guff.'

'He wouldn't dare.'

'You may remind him of that fact if the evening seems to be getting away from you.'

'I'm a tough copper, remember? I can handle any situation.'

'Like when Finn's owner talked you into buying him?'

'Don't talk about the boy like that; he doesn't like it. He almost went to some old fart who would have spoiled him rotten and ruined him.'

'He did.'

'You're funny.'

'I like to think so.' Eve winked at her husband.

'Good-looking and witty; what did I do in a previous life to deserve you?'

She laughed, and they finished their meal. Then Craig made coffees and they took them to the living room. The bridges were lit up again, off in the distance. Craig thought about telling Eve about the newspaper clippings, but that might spark a long conversation about them, and he didn't want to be late meeting Dan.

Then Craig's phone rang. It was his son.

'As if by magic, it's Joe,' Craig said to his wife. 'How do you do that? Next you'll be telling me you want a black cat.'

'Don't make me cast a spell on you. Just answer your phone.'

'Hello, son.'

'Hey, Dad. Would you make it for a pint tonight after all?'

'Absolutely. What made you change your mind?'

'Oh, I just felt bad, that's all. I'm looking forward to having a drink with you.'

'Great. I'm meeting a couple of colleagues at the Pitreavie Golf Club. I'm sure they wouldn't mind you joining us for a couple.'

'What time?'

'Seven.'

'That's fine, Dad. I'll have a swift one with you, then we'll have to shoot off. Previous engagement.'

'Oh, you're bringing your new girlfriend?'

'If that's okay?'

'That's fine. Make sure one of you isn't drinking and driving.'

'Yada-yada. Later, Dad.'

Joe disconnected the call, and Craig put his phone away, feeling like he had spared the rod and now this was the result.

'What did he say?' Eve asked.

'He's bringing the female along. And he said "yada-yada" when I told him not to drink and drive. He gets that from you.'

'Oh, does he now?' Eve said, raising her eyebrows. 'Nothing to do with you spoiling him when he was growing up?'

'Let's not let this get away from us,' Craig said, not wanting to take his irritation out on his wife.

'At least he's meeting up with you,' she said.

'Small mercies, eh?' He walked away to go and get changed.

TWENTY

Craig never liked to make an entrance at any place, being fashionably late or whatever else it was called. That was why he was fifteen minutes early at the golf club.

It seemed that Dan Stevenson had had the same idea. He was already standing at the bar nursing a pint. Craig walked up to him.

'A'right there, Jimmy?' Dan said, not turning round. Craig realised Dan had been watching him in the mirror behind the bar.

'Stop trying to act cool like you're Clint Eastwood or something. Go ahead, punk, get me a pint.'

Dan turned to look at Craig and shook his head. 'Acting school was burnt down when you got to London then? Decided to stick with the polis?'

'Hey, I could have been on TV, pal. With my looks and charisma? I would have knocked them dead.'

'What was that film called you were doing an audition for? *Illusions of Grandeur*, wasn't it?'

'Shut your hole. Lager, thanks.'

'Oh, here comes twinkletoes. Bacardi and Coke for her.' Dan gave the barman the order.

'I heard that,' Isla said, coming up behind them. 'Bloody twinkletoes.'

'I was talking about another twinkletoes,' Dan said in his defence.

'Yeah, yeah, save it for the judge.' She looked at Craig. 'We getting a table?'

Craig looked around. It was quiet; the hoards had not made their presence felt yet. 'Aye. Let's sit where we can face the door.' He looked at them. 'Listen, my boy, Joe, is coming along with his girlfriend. Just for a quick drink. He's at uni in St Andrews, and I don't see him often. Are you two okay with that? I can sit at a different table with him if you like.'

'Don't be daft,' Dan said. 'Of course it's okay.'

'Aye, that's fine, Jim,' Isla said.

They sat at a table against a wall, Craig keeping his eye on the door. They were chitchatting when the door to the lounge opened and Joe Craig walked in, followed by a woman.

Then the woman fished her phone out of her pocket and held it to her ear. Joe turned to look at her, and she held up a finger before leaving the lounge.

Joe looked puzzled as he walked over to where his father was sitting. 'Hi, Dad. Hi, folks,' he said to Isla and Dan.

'Hi, son. This is DS Isla McGregor and DS Dan Stevenson.'

The two detectives said hello as Craig stood up. 'Anybody ready for a chaser?'

'If you insist,' Dan said.

'Another Bacardi and Coke?' Craig asked Isla.

'Lovely, thanks.'

'Right, Joe, to the bar with me and you can help carry.'

Joe followed his father to the bar. 'Sorry about the confusion about coming out for a pint,' Joe said.

'Young love, eh?' Craig answered. 'What's her name?'

'Carrie. Dickson.'

'What is she drinking?'

'Just a Coke. She doesn't drink and drive. Unlike you and your cronies, apparently.'

'I got a taxi, and I'm not responsible for those two, but if I were a betting man, I'd say they didn't drive here. They live locally, so a taxi would be cheap.'

'Makes sense.'

Craig could sense a tension in the air with his son.

'What does Carrie do for a living?' Craig asked, paying the barman.

'She's a nurse. She goes to old people's houses to help with their medicine and the like.'

Craig nodded. 'Terrific occupation.'

Joe nodded. 'Sorry about her answering the phone. She tends to unwind just a bit too much when off duty. Not drugs or anything, but she gets goofy and clowns around a lot.'

'There are worse things in life, son.'

'I know,' Joe said, 'like waking up in the morning with a rash.'

'Here, cut that out. Don't be talking like that in front of the lassie.'

'I'm kidding, Dad. It's not like I woke up with a rash,' Joe said, accepting the pint from his dad and grabbing Carrie's Coke. Craig grabbed the rest.

'You're a grown man. I don't want to hear the

details, and I'd better not hear you talking like that in front of your mother.'

'Yeah, like that would happen. The name's Crafty, not Dafty.'

'That's debatable.'

They sat down again.

'Cheers, Jim,' Dan said. Isla raised her glass in a salute.

'You're hanging out with a couple of old fogeys on a Friday night?' Joe said to Isla.

'Do you think everybody over thirty is an old fogey?' Isla said, smiling.

Joe laughed. 'No, no, just kidding. I was surprised to see somebody as young as yourself in a golf club bar on a Friday instead of being over in Edinburgh dancing the night away.'

'Those days are past now, I think,' she said.

Dan looked at Isla, ignoring the old fogeys jibe. 'Nonsense. Your life's just starting. When you get to my age, it's time to sit in a golf club drinking cheap booze. And by cheap, I mean the prices.'

They looked round as Carrie approached, her eyes red, like she'd been crying. 'Sorry about that. It was a friend of mine from work. My grandfather just died. He was taken to the Victoria.'

'That's the hospital where she works,' Joe explained to Craig.

'Aye, I know that place.' He looked at Carrie and stood up. 'Sorry to hear that, Carrie. I'm Joe's dad, Jim. These are my colleagues from Police Scotland, Isla and Dan.'

She nodded to them, took a paper handkerchief out of her pocket and dabbed at her eyes. Craig nudged his son to stand up. Joe nodded and stood up from the table.

'Was your grandfather ill, Carrie?' Craig asked.

Carrie shook her head. 'No. He lives with me.' She looked at Craig. 'He fell down the stairs and died.'

TWENTY-ONE

Craig sipped his pint and looked at Dan and Isla. 'You thinking what I'm thinking?' He had waited until Joe and Carrie left before making the remark.

Isla looked him in the eye. 'You think Eve's uncle was murdered. That's why you had me at your house running through the scenario of whether it would have been possible or not for somebody to sneak out of a room and push him down the stairs. We discovered it was. Now you hear of another old man falling down the stairs, and you're wondering whether he could have been murdered as well.'

Craig nodded. 'Yes, I am.' He looked at Dan. 'I found a bag of lollipops in a nook in Clark's house.'

'Lollipops?' Isla said. 'Clark wouldn't eat lollipops. He had diabetes.'

'His cleaner told me that Clark had a lot of newspaper clippings about the killing of a detective twenty-five years ago, DS Stuart Hunt. I was with him the night he was murdered. The killer attacked me, and Dan here ran up, screaming like a banshee, shouting out threats to him just as he was about to kill me. He'd smacked me in the head with something, and I couldn't defend myself. Dan saved me. Clark was a detective then, while Dan and I were in uniform. I think the case must have bugged him, even into retirement. But there's one key element in this whole case.'

'What's that?' Isla asked.

'Lollipops,' Dan said.

'Christ, just saying it out loud makes it seem stupid. *The Lollipop Killer*. How does that sound to you?' Craig asked Isla.

'Like something out of a comic book.'

'Exactly. But that's what I think has been happening ever since that night. Maybe even before it. This killer is murdering people and leaving a lollipop at each scene. Some killers leave signatures for the police to find, but we think this guy just leaves a lollipop as his signature without the police noticing.'

Isla looked at Dan. 'This is what you think too?'

Dan nodded, then looked at Craig, who nodded in understanding. Craig looked Isla in the eye. 'When the killer was about to ram his weapon into my eyeball, I saw it was a lollipop stick. He was holding the lollipop in his hand and was about to kill me with it. I later thought I'd been seeing things and wrote in my report that it was a knife blade. But today, I spoke to Dan, and he saw the stick too. He didn't contradict my report at the time, thinking he must have been mistaken. Now I think Clark figured out what's been happening all these years and bought the bag of lollipops to take one and confront the killer. I don't know if he did, but there was a lollipop in his belongings that the funeral director sent back home with my wife. And I think the old man was pushed down the stairs.'

'And now you think this might have happened to Carrie's grandfather?' Isla said.

'I don't know, but I'm sure that if we were to go to the house, there would be a lollipop somewhere in there. Sitting there, unnoticed, because the families are usually too grief-stricken to even notice. And later on, even if they find it, they don't question it. And the killer gets away again.'

Isla sipped her drink. 'Jesus. You think he's been killing for over twenty-five years?'

'Yes.'

'And getting away with it,' Dan added. 'And nobody's stopping him.'

'How long do you think he's been doing this?' Isla asked.

'A very long time,' Craig said. 'I think he'd started it before the night he attacked me, but that night he very nearly got caught.'

Dan looked at Craig. 'Let's assume we give him an average age of twenty when he started –'

Craig held up a hand. 'No, Dan, I was inches away from him. All I could see were his eyes. But he was no twenty-year-old. Not old either, but I want to say, a little mature. More towards mid- to late-twenties.'

'Okay, mid- to late-twenties. Add twenty-five years to that. He'd be fifty-plus, maybe. That's the age group we should be looking at.'

'We don't have a suspect, though, do we?' Isla said.

'I think Clark did. Somebody ripped the newspaper clippings off his study wall, clippings his cleaner saw. I found them stuffed into his recycling bin. I'm going to go through them and see if I can find anything. Maybe he had notes written down.'

'I wish he had told one of us,' Dan said.

Craig looked at him. 'I think it was just a theory he was working on, but unfortunately for him, he decided to confront the killer and the guy murdered him, making it look like an accident. He seems quite confident that he can walk about undetected.'

'Maybe you should go and have a look at Carrie's grandfather's house later when she gets home.'

'I will,' Craig said. 'Do either of you two have DCI Mickey Thompson's phone number? I want to get in touch with him about Clark.'

'I have it,' Isla said. 'He wanted me to be his emergency contact since his wife died. He has no family.'

She gave it to Craig.

'I'll try calling him in the morning.'

'I don't think there's much mobile service up there,' Dan said. 'At least that's what Mickey said. I think he switches his phone off, like Clark did, and they'd sit around gambling and getting blootered. Sometimes they would go for a hike, so he said, but I think walking was the last thing on their minds.'

'Do you know where the cottage is?' Craig said.

'No. Clark and Mickey would sometimes go up

together for fishing. And getting pished of course. Mickey went there after getting a kicking. Said he'll be back down for Christmas.'

'Who gave him a kicking?' Craig asked.

'Your guess is as good as ours. He didn't see it coming. He was mugged, he said, but nothing was taken, so unless he was mugged by the Tooth Fairy, I think he was pished and fell down the stairs on his own.'

Craig and Isla were silent. Dan looked at them in turn. 'You don't think...?'

'We'll have to talk to him about that,' Craig said. 'I have to go over to Edinburgh tomorrow to see a friend of mine, but I can go up on Sunday. If either of you want to come?'

'I can make it,' Dan said.

'Me too,' Isla told Craig.

'Great. How about we meet about eleven?'

'There's only one thing,' Dan said. 'We don't know the exact address of the cottage.'

'You're a detective, Dan. You can use your resources to find out. Unless my wife has the address. I'll call you if she has it; otherwise, I'll see you Sunday.'

'Meet here in the car park?' Dan suggested.

'Fine. We can take my car,' Craig said.

They had another few drinks and then got the barman to call for two taxis, Dan sharing with Isla. Craig was thinking about another old man lying at the foot of his stairs. It was getting out of control now.

TWENTY-TWO

'Did you see Joe?' Eve asked as Finn rubbed himself against Craig's legs.

'For a little while. And Carrie. She's very nice. She's a nurse and she lives in Kirkcaldy with her grandfather.' Craig calmed the dog down and sat on the chair in the living room. Eve was sprawled out on the couch like she'd been at the cooking sherry.

'What about this thing with answering his phone?'

'He apologised. She gets a bit carried away at times, relieving stress. You should know all about that with teaching those little bastards.'

'Don't call them that,' Eve protested but with a smile on her face.

'You have them when they're young and I deal with them when they get older.'

'Anything else about Carrie?'

'Yes. Her grandfather died tonight. They found him at the bottom of the stairs.'

Eve was silent, looking over at her husband. 'I feel like you want to say something to me.'

'I think he was murdered.'

'Good God, Jim, what makes you say that?'

'Listen, this isn't easy for me to say, but I think Clark was murdered too.' He expected her to take a sharp breath, or ask him in a raised voice why the hell he was saying such a thing. Tears maybe, or shouting at the very least, tell him he was a slavering arsehole. But none of that happened, and he thought for a moment that he'd broken his wife. Maybe he'd have to open up a socket and stick one of her fingers in it. He didn't know if they had smelling salts or not (leaning towards the "not") and he looked at her face to see if she had heard him the first time.

'I said –' Craig started to say, but Eve interrupted him.

'I know.' The dog came over and she petted him. 'I mean, I know what you mean when you say you think he was murdered. I think so too.'

He leaned forward in the chair, sliding on the

slippery leather. 'You do? What makes you think that? So we can compare notes.'

'Being married to a copper makes you think differently. Damn you, James Craig, you've got me suspicious about everything. Every bloody thing in life, I second-guess. But don't worry, I'm not blaming you.' She smiled at him and he could see tears in her eyes now.

'I was in the study,' she said, 'when I saw the papers in the bin liner. I was curious, so I looked inside, and there they were: newspaper clippings about Stuart Hunt's murder. The night you almost died. If that big, beautiful man called Dan Stevenson hadn't come running, we wouldn't be sitting here having this conversation. I wouldn't even be a widow, because we weren't married at the time.'

'You'd be sitting here with a rich banker or something,' Craig said.

'It's not funny, Craig. A little piece of me died inside that night when I got told. Your dad came to my house and took me to the hospital to see you. I felt like my insides had been scooped out, and I never want to feel that way again.'

'I'm sorry.'

'But you recovered from being bashed on the head and I got married to a copper and now I always see the worst in people until I get to know them better. I see a mugger when other people see somebody merely walking for a train. I don't trust anybody right off the bat. They have to prove themselves to be trustworthy. All because of you, and I don't say that in a mean way. Now, back to Clark: he sent me a text message a week before he died.'

'What did it say?' he asked.

'He said, if anything happens to me, remember this. And he sent me a photo.'

'A photo of what?' He looked at her, waiting for an answer, but he knew the answer.

'A lollipop.'

He nodded slowly, not saying anything.

'I thought it was weird,' Eve said, 'but then I saw the bag of lollipops here, and the one that was in his possessions the funeral director gave us. Now I'm convinced that he was murdered. It was almost like he knew his killer. Does that make sense?'

'Yes, it does. I have the same feeling but for different reasons than you.'

'Help me understand, Jimmy.'

So he told her. All of it.

When he was finished, she got up, walked over to him and knelt, ignoring the dog, and she leaned into him. He held her as she cried. After the sobbing subsided, he still held on to her.

Later, she moved away from him and looked him in the eye. 'You're going to get the bastard, Jimmy?'

'I've already started.'

It was late when Craig and Eve arrived at Carrie's house in Kirkcaldy. She was visibly shaken, and not even Joe being with her could console her. Craig was aware that he could be walking into a crime scene and was careful what he touched. He'd told Eve to keep her hands in her pockets.

'Carrie, this is my mum, Eve,' Joe said.

'Hello,' Carrie replied, dabbing at her eyes. 'Sorry, I'm a complete mess.'

'There's no need to be sorry,' Eve replied, sitting on the couch beside her.

The house was modern, detached, on a quiet street. Craig noticed the Zimmer walking frame out in the hallway, where he presumed the old man had been found.

He walked along to a door that led to the kitchen and stepped inside, hitting the light switch. It was painted in a shade of white with white cabinets. He walked over to the countertop and looked around, eyes scanning for one thing – a lollipop. There wasn't one that he could see.

Maybe it was an accident after all. Older people were sometimes a bit unsteady on their feet. Maybe Grandpa had a few drinks and decided to try to go to bed early. He got to the top of the hill before tumbling back down, and all the King's men couldn't bring him back to life. *It happens,* he thought, annoyed at himself for jumping to conclusions.

But he reminded himself that this might be too much of a coincidence – first Eve's uncle and now Joe's girlfriend's grandfather.

He found a glass in a cupboard and poured some cold water into it, his excuse for coming through to the kitchen. He returned and gave it to Carrie, who looked at it like it might have been neat vodka. Hoping it was, maybe.

'It's water,' Craig explained, and he was sure he could see disappointment on her face, but she sipped some of it anyway before putting it down on the coffee table.

'Thank you,' she said.

'They took him to Victoria,' Craig said.

Carrie nodded. 'Yes. It's the only accident and emergency now.'

Craig looked at Eve for confirmation, and she nodded. 'Politicians,' she said.

'How did I not know that?' he said.

Joe just shrugged, like his father had asked him where he'd got the magazines his mother had found under the bed.

'Was he pronounced dead there?' Craig asked Carrie.

She nodded. 'The paramedics said he had a faint pulse, but by the time he got there, he was gone.'

'What was your grandfather's name?'

'Albert Duncan.'

'Did Albert often go up the stairs on his own?'

Carrie whipped her head around to look at him. 'Oh God, no. He used his Zimmer to walk around. He couldn't manage the stairs without great difficulty.'

'Any idea why he would go up there tonight on his own? Maybe he wanted to go to bed, and there was nobody around to help him?' Craig said, then realised this sounded critical. He softened the blow. 'I know you have a life of your own. You can't be here twenty-four seven.'

'No, his bedroom was down here. I converted my dining room for him.'

'How long had he lived here with you?' Craig asked.

'He was getting frailer so he moved in with me last summer.'

'What about the bathroom, love?' Eve said, putting a hand on Carrie's.

Craig looked at Carrie, wondering if she would one day be his daughter-in-law or if it was too early to start thinking like this.

'There's a downstairs bathroom along the hall. He never had to go upstairs. I have a baby monitor in his room, so if he needed me, all he had to do was shout, and I'd come running.'

'What about when you were at work?' Craig asked. 'Did anybody look in on him?'

'My next-door neighbour, Agnes. She and her husband are in their sixties, but they're so good about popping in now and again. Plus, I have patients in the area, so I come home when there's a fair bit of time between a couple of them. He was quite spry, apart from having bad knees and arthritis.'

'Something made him go upstairs,' Craig said, realising that he was again using the same tone he'd use with some hooligan sitting across the table from him in an interview room.

'I can't imagine what,' Carrie said.

Craig made a mental note to ask Dan to pull up the police report from the uniforms and also to see what time the triple-nine call was logged.

'Who found him?' he asked.

'Agnes did. I asked her if she would mind popping in when I was out with Joe.' Carrie looked at Craig. 'It's not as if I don't help her out. Her husband's been in and out of hospital, so I help change his bandages, or I go in and feed their cat. We help each other out. I asked her to pop her head in and make up his hot water bottle. He always liked his hot water bottle in bed.'

'Does she have a key?'

Carrie nodded. 'Yes. She let herself in and found him lying there.'

Craig knew a report would be sent to the procurator fiscal, and depending on what answer the pathologist came up with after the postmortem, they would go from there.

Then a thought struck him. 'Did they give you his clothes to bring home?' he asked Carrie.

'Yes, in a plastic bag.'

'Would you mind if I looked through them?'

'No, that would be fine. Can I ask why, though?'

'I just wanted to see if he had keys on him.' Craig hoped she wouldn't see through the lie.

'Oh, right. The bag's over there.' She nodded towards a chair on the opposite side of the room.

He picked up the bag, put it on the chair, and opened it, looking inside. He made sure his back was to Carrie when he started going through Albert's things. There was underwear and socks, a shirt, a cardigan, and shoes, but Craig was most interested in the trousers.

He pulled on a pair of nitrile gloves, hoping Carrie wouldn't ask why, but God bless Eve, she kept her talking and distracted. He lifted the trousers a bit, put his hand in the right pocket and found the keys. He let them go. The left-hand pocket contained a wallet. And a long, thin thing. He felt his heart rate increase and delved deeper, touching a ball shape. He pulled it out and looked at what it was, what he was expecting to find in the kitchen but didn't.

A lollipop.

Christ, he thought. The killer had been in here and had ended Albert's life. Maybe he'd taken the old boy up the stairs by force. He'd get Dan to call the pathologist and have them look for bruising like Albert had been banged about.

The doorbell rang, and Craig returned the lollipop and removed the gloves. 'The keys are there,' he said, leaving the living room.

He answered the door, opening it up and letting the cold night in.

DSup Mark Baker was standing in front of him. His cheeks were flushed like he'd been running, but with his extra weight, Craig doubted the man could run a bath.

'Jimmy? What are you doing here?'

'Carrie's my son's girlfriend.' Craig made no move to let the man in.

'I knew Albert. I couldn't believe it when I got told.' Baker moved forward, and Craig stepped aside. He was bigger than the superintendent, and since he wasn't a member of Police Scotland, he could have said anything he wanted to the man, but he merely let him in without further ado.

Baker walked into the living room and saw Carrie sitting on the couch.

'Hello, Carrie. Eve.'

Eve looked at the man like she'd just downed a couple of vodkas and was now deciding between puking or singing. 'You have the advantage,' she said, neither throwing up nor bursting into "I Will Survive", her karaoke speciality.

'Detective Superintendent Mark Baker,' Craig said. 'But apparently, you know my wife.'

'Clark spoke fondly of her,' Baker said, turning towards Craig. Then, back to Eve. 'My condolences.'

'Thank you.'

'You too, Carrie. I couldn't believe it when I heard about Bert.'

'Thanks, Mark.'

'You must be Joe. Pleased to meet you, son.'

'Likewise.'

'What a right to-do. I only saw him last week.' Baker turned to Craig again. 'Bert liked his wee nip and a game of dominoes. Not darts, though; his hand shook like it had been sitting on a jackhammer. He would have had somebody's eye out.'

'How did you find out he was dead?'

'I was in the office working late when one of my uniforms came in and told me. He knew Bert and I go way back.'

'Clark was a good man,' Carrie said. 'Taken too soon.'

'Aye, I miss the old boy. Like I'll miss Bert.'

'That's very nice, Mark.'

'Would you like a cup of tea or anything?' Eve said. 'I was about to put the kettle on.'

'Aye. Ta. That would be very much appreciated.' Baker took his overcoat off and made himself at home.

Eve got up and went through to the kitchen, Joe following her.

Craig sat down on the couch. 'How did you know Bert?' he asked.

Baker gave a grim smile. 'Bert was one of us, Jimmy. He was a retired copper. He was my mentor, back in the day. I learned a lot from him and he didn't mind taking the time to teach me. I would come round here and we'd have a gab about the old days.' His mind went elsewhere momentarily, and Craig thought the older man had gone into a trance or something. Then Baker snapped back to the here and now.

'I hope you had a mentor down there in that pit they call a city, Jimmy.'

'I did. A Scotsman as it turned out.'

'I'm glad. People are too quick to dismiss older people, but they're living history. Just take the time to sit and listen to them and you'll learn a lot.'

'That's true,' Craig said. 'Of course, I didn't get the chance to talk to my father when he got old, because he died young.'

'Aye, you never know what's around the corner, Jimmy. Live each day as if it's going to be your last, that's what I say. My wife ran out on me a long time ago, and I've never heard from her since, but you know what? I couldn't care less. We're only here once, so make the most of it. Isn't that right, Carrie?'

'That's true, Mark.'

Craig didn't think that Baker's philosophy was helping Carrie just then.

'How long have you been seeing...' Baker paused for a second as if he couldn't remember Joe's name, and he used his thumb to point towards the kitchen. Either that or he had slipped back into his trance and was now thumbing a lift on the A82.

'Joe,' Craig said, filling in the blank.

'Aye. The young stud through there.'

'About three months,' Carrie answered.

Baker raised his eyebrows, and Craig realised that the man wasn't having mini strokes but that he had been drinking. He was good at masking it, that was for sure, but whatever alcohol he'd consumed was slowly working on his brain.

'Three months, you say. Bert didn't mention it.'

Carrie sniffed and dabbed at her eyes again. 'He didn't? Maybe he forgot.'

'Aye, let's give the old codger the benefit of the doubt.'

'Did you ever play dominoes with Clark?' Craig asked Baker.

'Clark? No, he wasn't interested in that stuff. He

and Thompson were always skulking about together. Thompson even came along here from time to time, didn't he?' The question was directed at Carrie.

'What? Oh yes, Mickey came along to hang out with Granddad sometimes. It was almost like a network the retired coppers had.'

'Except Thompson isn't retired. I think he would like to be and he's not a kick in the balls off it, but now he's off somewhere pretending to be retired.'

'What happened to him?' Craig asked, wondering where Eve was with the fucking tea. Baker was a slavering bastard and the quicker they had their tea, the faster he would be out of here. Craig wasn't going to leave first, not with Joe here. He wouldn't do that to his son, leave him in the company of a man who would bore a hostage taker into submission. Maybe they were going to be in for a long night. Maybe if time went on and there was no sign of Baker leaving, Craig could borrow a pair of Bert's pyjamas and slippers, and see if Baker would take the hint.

'I heard Mickey Thompson got a kicking,' he said. Baker looked round at him, his eyes slightly glazed over, and Craig thought the man had had more to drink than he'd first thought. Baker was looking at him like he didn't remember who he was now. Then the light in his eyes danced a bit and recognition kicked in. It was almost as if he'd downed a half bottle before coming in and the alcohol was starting to grip him.

'It wasn't quite a kicking. He was following up on a line of enquiry, and somebody smacked him. Knocked him out.'

'Did you get anybody for it?'

'Phhff. Got to be fucking joking.' Baker put a hand up to his mouth and looked at Carrie. 'Sorry about the French there, sweetheart. But no, whoever skelped him got away. I got called out and I got a load of uniforms to do a door-to-door, but it wasn't in the most salubrious part of town, if you know what I mean. They saw nothing, they heard nothing, and that was from the ones who opened their door. Some of them even opened their door and took great delight in telling my boys and girls to piss off. We didn't get anybody, and Thompson went on sick leave. There was more to it, though. I'm not supposed to discuss it.'

He looked at Craig and Carrie in turn. 'Oh, go on, you wore me down.'

Craig put up a hand. 'If it's personal, it's best not to.'

Baker laughed. 'Shite. Thompson would be the

first to tell you if we were in the pub. He's going a bit loopy.' Baker blew a raspberry and spun a finger at his right temple. 'Loco-motion, if you know what I mean. Poor bastard. Don't get me wrong, I've never been one of his drinking buddies, but I like the guy. I'm sure they're going to farm him out one day. He's been going off the rails for a long time now.'

Carrie looked puzzled. 'Has he? Granddad never said anything.'

'He's good at hiding it. Like an alky.'

Well, you would know, Craig thought. 'Is he getting help?'

'He goes to see a shrink. Or at least, he's supposed to. Bill Walker would know more about that, I suppose.'

'I've been trying to get hold of Mickey,' Craig said. 'To let him know about Clark.'

'He said something about going to the wee cottage that he owns. He and Clark would go poncing about up there, fishing and hiking, he said, but I think they went there to play cards and get blootered every day.'

'Do you know the exact address?'

Baker shrugged. 'Somewhere up north. He never told me exactly where it was and I'm not interested. It's not like I'm getting invited up there anytime soon, and if I were, I'd tell him to shove it up his hole. I don't want the fucking neighbours thinking –'

'Tea's up!' Eve said, walking into the living room, followed by Joe carrying a tray with mugs on it.

'We couldn't find the teapot,' Joe said.

'I don't have one,' Carrie said.

'That would explain it.'

'We did find a wee milk jug and a sugar bowl.' Eve told Joe to put the tray on the coffee table, and Carrie moved her glass of water.

'You'll make somebody a good wife one day, Eve,' Baker said, looking at Craig and winking, smirking to himself.

'Well, he'd better be bloody rich!' Eve said, giggling.

Baker thought this was the funniest thing he'd ever heard and laughed. 'Hear that, Craigie? You're bumped if she finds somebody who's just won the lottery.'

'I'll take that risk.'

Then all the hilarity left Baker, as it often did with some drunks. 'You know, it wasn't that long ago that Bert and I were sitting in this very living room, swapping war stories.' He looked at Carrie. 'You have to be one of us to get it. Some coppers only have other coppers as friends; they never have friends outside the force. That sums up Thompson.'

'But he had Granddad and Clark as friends,' Carrie said.

'Ex-coppers. He wouldn't have been friends with them if they were ex-miners. Or bus drivers. They all had something in common. But I don't think even Bert and Clark could help Thompson fight his demons.' Baker sipped his tea and looked around for a plate of biscuits, saw none and screwed his face up. 'If you ask me, I don't think Thompson will be back on duty. He'll have to go and see the force psychologist and I doubt he'll be deemed fit to return to work. They'd be better pensioning him off before he lamps a member of the public and embarrasses the high heid yins.'

'You think he would do that?' Craig asked.

Baker slurped more tea, and Craig thought that maybe Thompson shouldn't be the only one the chief constable was watching.

'Fucking hot,' Baker complained, blowing across the surface. He looked at Craig like he was trying to decipher the question. 'Oh. Aye. I think Thompson would fly off the handle and give somebody a skelping.'

'Except the person who knocked him out.'

'He was sucker-punched. I'm sure he would have put up a good fight if he hadn't been, but would he have been able to restrain himself if he got going? It's like a switch gets flicked in his brain and off he goes. I'm going to push for his retirement. He deserves to go out with his money intact, not being shown the door because the stress got the better of him.' He blew on the tea again and looked at Craig as if to say, *Watch my back. I'm going in.* Then he sipped the tea again.

Eve looked at him. 'I must say, my uncle never said anything about Mickey getting angry.'

'He wouldn't, would he? Thompson didn't show his anger around his friends, no doubt. It was just the great unwashed. Or maybe he did let go at them and they never said anything.'

'He never did it here with Granddad, at least not when I was in the house,' Carrie said.

'He was good at covering it. But he needs our help now,' Baker said, giving up on the blowing and reaching for the little jug of milk instead. He poured it in with a shaky hand.

'Where does Mickey live?' Craig asked.

'Bowhill.'

Craig knew this was near Cardenden, maybe

fifteen minutes away. 'Have you tried going to his house? In case he didn't go to the cottage?'

'I did. It's empty. His next-door neighbour said he'd been away for days now. The old bloke said he couldn't remember exactly when he left.'

Baker put his tea down and stood up. 'I need to visit the wee man's room. If you know what I mean.'

Carrie nodded and they watched Baker leave the living room.

'Looks like he's been out on the lash,' Joe said.

'It seems that Granddad and Clark dying has hit him hard,' Carrie said, looking at the doorway that Baker had just gone through. 'Grief hits people in different ways. I know that from the old people I work with.'

A few minutes later, Baker came back. 'I'll be off. Carrie, sorry once again for your loss.'

Craig was expecting the older detective to be slurring his words by now, but he wasn't.

'You need a lift anywhere?' Craig asked.

'Nah. Thanks anyway. Taxis are coming up from the hospital. I'll be fine.'

They watched Baker leave like a magician who'd just completed his final act.

'I thought he'd never go,' Craig said.

'He's okay,' Carrie said. 'Granddad was always pleased to see him.'

'Aye, I suppose.' Craig looked at his watch. 'We'd best be going,' he said to Eve.

'I'll just clear up first,' she said.

'No, you won't. Joe will do that, eh, son?'

'Yes, Dad.'

Craig and Eve stood up.

'Nice to meet you, Carrie,' Eve said as Carrie stood. They hugged, and then Carrie turned to Craig and hugged him too.

'Maybe you and Joe could come round to the house and have a bite to eat before we head back home. Meet Finn. He loves meeting new people,' Eve said.

'I'd like that.'

Craig thought about the lollipop that had been in Albert's pocket and felt that it couldn't possibly be a coincidence.

He decided he would keep it to himself for the moment.

They got in the car and drove away. There was no sign of Mark Baker.

TWENTY-THREE

Saturday brought snow to Fife like somebody had laid a white blanket over everything.

'Three weeks too early for a white Christmas,' Craig said, standing in the small sitting area in the living room, looking out over to the bridges in the distance. The water looked cold and uninviting. He watched a plane on its final approach to Edinburgh Airport as it headed towards Cramond on the Edinburgh side. He sipped the coffee he'd made. Finn was lying at his feet, having followed him from the kitchen. The dog had got out of bed after Craig had showered and followed him around.

He ran the events of the previous night through his head. Carrie's grandfather had been found dead just like Clark had been, and the old boy had a lollipop in his trousers. Christ, even thinking about it now made him cringe. How could he go to the high heid yins and give them his theory of how he thought somebody was killing people and leaving his mark behind? Thank God Dan had seen Craig's attacker with the lollipop in his hand. Otherwise, it would make his theory seem like a children's story.

Eve walked into the living room, yawning and stretching, still in her pyjamas. Finn got up, wagging his tail, and went over to her like he hadn't seen her in days.

'Hey, pal,' she said, rubbing the dog's head.

Craig turned towards her. 'The kettle's not long off. You want me to make you a coffee?'

'No, you're going out. I'll do it myself.'

Craig sipped more of his coffee. 'Dan and I are going to go to Mickey's cottage, but we can't find the address.'

'Clark mentioned going there before, but I don't know where it is. Somewhere in Perthshire, I think.'

'Christ, that narrows it down,' he said, his voice laced with anger, but he wasn't angry with his wife. 'Sorry, love. I'm pissed off that somebody killed your uncle and the bastard is still out there.'

'If he was indeed murdered. There's no proof, Jimmy.'

'I have to get going. I'm meeting with Harry McNeil over in Edinburgh. Then Angie Fisher is coming through from Glasgow to see how Olivia fares walking outside the hospital again. She's been out before but I want to be there when she goes out again.'

'Which reminds me, why would The Hammer send Clark a photo of a hammer?'

'I think that message was for me. That's why he sent one to Olivia and her father. He's playing games with me. I think he knew I was coming up here, so he sent those first, then one to Barry Norman, to make sure I would see it. He knows a lot more about me than I know about him.'

'I'm worried he'll try to get to you, Jimmy.'

'If he does, I'll be waiting. He's just killed a woman, and that means if he sticks to his pattern, it'll be a while before he kills again.'

'He didn't send photos to people you know before, did he?' Eve asked.

Craig shook his head. 'No. But don't worry, I'll be alert. Keep the door locked, and if big boy there starts barking make sure you know who's at the door first before you answer.'

'I will.'

Craig kissed his wife, grabbed his jacket and car

keys, and went downstairs to the garage. He took a broom and went out to his car, locking the door behind him. The Volvo was covered in snow, and he used the broom to wipe it off. He tossed the broom in the back and got the car started.

The seats were freezing, but the heaters soon warmed them up, and the roads had been taken care of. It hadn't been a huge snowstorm, and the drive across to Edinburgh was easy. It took him around half an hour to get along to Morningside. He decided to park in the car park of the Royal Ed and walk round to the café on Morningside Road. There was no snow in Edinburgh, like Fife had been singled out to be dumped on.

The café was on the corner of Canaan Lane and was a decent size, with a few tables and a counter facing the door. A bell chimed as he walked in. He saw a couple sitting by one wall, and the man waved at him. He stood up as Craig approached.

'So much for my stealth,' he said. 'Trying not to look like a copper and failing miserably.' His first thought was that this might be The Hammer and he was prepared to pepper-spray the bastard with the little canister he kept in his pocket, then lamp him one on the chin, but before he got close enough, the man smiled and held out his hand.

'DCI Harry McNeil. My wife, DS Alex McNeil.'

Craig shook Harry's hand, and then Alex's. 'Can I get you a top-up?' he asked Harry.

'Americano, cheers.'

'Same, Jimmy, thanks,' Alex said, smiling.

'If you order something, the woman will bring it to you,' Harry said. 'We've already had a bacon roll, but you fire in if you're hungry.'

'I only had a coffee for breakfast, so I might as well rip up my Weight Watchers membership card now.'

'You're hardly a chunk, Jimmy,' Harry said.

'Try telling that to the wife. She's thinking of buying me a gym membership for Christmas, but I told her I'd rather have my subscription to Netflix renewed.'

'I hear that,' Harry said.

Craig ordered the coffees and a bacon roll, and as Harry had promised, the woman said she would bring them over.

'Nice place,' he said, sitting down at the table.

'We've been here a few times,' Alex said.

'I appreciate you meeting me here today. And for getting Angie Fisher on board.'

'No problem. It's a shame Olivia's had to spend

so much time in that place,' Harry said. 'When you told me on the phone, I couldn't believe it. It's just like being in prison. How long has she been in there now?'

'Almost five years. Only recently, she's been going out with a nurse, trying to regain her self-confidence. I'm hunting a killer in London the press has nicknamed *The Hammer*.' Craig explained about the photos that had been sent to Olivia and her father, and the one sent to Clark.

'There was a message on the back of Olivia's, daring her to come out. And the postmark was Edinburgh. He either got it sent here to be posted or he travelled up from London.'

'That's awful,' Alex said.

'That's why I just wanted the Edinburgh team to know the score. I'm up here for Clark's funeral, but I won't be up here for good.'

'I can have one of my team keep an eye on Olivia,' Harry said, as the woman came across with the coffees and the roll.

'Thank you,' Craig said.

'I'm sure Olivia's father would appreciate that.' Craig bit into the bacon roll, savouring the ketchup and the warm butter. Of course, he'd tell Eve that he hadn't eaten any such thing, and she would look at him with her *lying bastard* look, but without any proof, she would have to find him *not guilty*.

'Does he live close by?' Alex asked.

'No, in Glasgow. He's a psychiatrist, like Olivia was until her patient attacked her.'

'She doesn't have anybody close by then?' Harry asked.

'No. She's all alone here in Edinburgh apart from the hospital staff.'

'Jeez, that's such a shame,' Alex said. 'I could keep in touch with her too. Angie and I.'

'I'm sure she would love that,' Craig said, taking another bite of his roll.

'Did Harry mention that I was with Fife MIT until a few weeks ago?'

Craig shook his head in reply as he was still eating.

'I was going to mention it,' Harry said to his wife. 'You didn't give me a chance.'

Craig washed the roll down with the rest of his coffee. 'What made you leave?'

'I got an offer to work with the Scottish government, so I took it. A colleague and I were transferred. It was a good opportunity.'

'That's terrific.'

Harry's phone rang and he took it out. After

looking at the screen, he excused himself, stepping out into the cold.

'You met on the job, I take it? If I'm not being too nosy,' Craig said.

'We did. I worked in the cold case unit, and Harry came along to work on a case. We met at the station. Long story. But my new role is more of a desk job than a field officer.'

'Whatever's best for you.' Craig saw a text come up on his smartwatch. 'That's Angie round at the hospital now. I should get going.'

Just then, Harry came back in and leaned over at the table. 'That was Charlie Skellett. There was an explosion at a house in South Gyle last night. Suspected gas leak. I have to go over there.' He looked at Craig. 'Charlie's my DI.'

Both Craig and Alex knew it had to be serious if Harry was being called out to the scene.

'I could go with Jim here,' Alex said to Harry. 'If that's okay with you, Jim?'

'Of course. I'll introduce you to Olivia. The more friendly faces she sees, the better. Not that the staff are bad, but if she knows somebody else can take her out and that person is also a police officer, I'm sure that will help her.'

'That's it settled then. I'll see you later, Harry.'

'How will you get home?' he asked her.

'I'll get a taxi.'

'I'll drive you home,' Craig said.

'You don't know where we live,' she said with a smile. 'It could be miles out of town.'

'I'm not in a hurry to get home. My wife is preparing for her uncle's funeral on Monday and she won't want me under her feet. It's bad enough the dog will want her attention.'

Alex laughed. 'We live in Murrayfield. It's on your way home, sort of. If you take a detour, that is.'

They stood up.

'Thanks, pal,' Harry said, shaking Craig's hand.

'Anytime. And thanks again for making this happen.'

'We'll need to have a pint one night and you can fill in all the blanks about Olivia.'

'I'll give you a call.'

'I've heard that before,' Harry said, smiling and patting Craig on the arm.

'Not recently, I hope,' Alex said, raising one eyebrow.

'All the time,' Harry said, winking at her.

'Liar.' She looked at Craig. 'He always has this little look on his face when he's trying to pull the wool over my eyes.'

Harry held out his hands as if to say, *You got me.*

'Catch you later, Jimmy. See you at home, honey.'

'Gotcha.'

Harry paid the bill and then walked out, the little bell ringing again, and Alex grabbed her jacket off the back of her chair and put it on.

'I would have got the bill,' Craig said.

'Trust me, when Harry offers to pay the bill, don't argue. It doesn't happen that often.'

Craig laughed and they made the bell above the door ding again. Craig wondered how many times a day the bell would have to ring before the woman behind the counter considered bringing a firearm to work.

It was a five-minute walk round to the hospital car park, ten if it was icy and there was a risk of one of them going on their arse, but they were off to a good start.

'I just thought, here's me calling you Jimmy when you're a DCI and I'm only a sergeant,' Alex said.

'I'm with the Met, and I'm meeting you here as a friend today. I promise I won't write about you on Instagram. They'd be baying for your blood for such insubordination.'

'It would set the internet on fire.'

'I'll bet you want to call DCI Fisher by her first name too?' he said as they crossed the road.

'I've already spoken to her today, so that's a given.'

'Good. Then we'll all be on first-name terms.'

'Seriously, though, what does Olivia call you?'

'I make her call me *sir*.'

Alex looked at him. 'No way.'

He laughed. 'No way.'

'My opinion of you was about to change,' she said, wincing.

'You okay?' Craig asked her.

'I am, thanks. It's just that somebody ran me off the road weeks ago and I'm having pain in my shoulder.'

'How bad was it? The crash?'

'Harry's Audi was written off and I got a smashed nose, but it could have been a lot worse.'

'They got the guy, I hope,' Craig said as they entered the car park.

'Yes, they did. An armed response team took them down.'

'Good.'

They saw a woman climb out of her car into the cold morning air, pulling on a woollen hat over her blonde hair pulled back into a ponytail. DCI Angie Fisher waved to them, and they reached her car just as she was locking it.

'I wasn't sure how far it was,' she said.

'It's just a short drive round the corner to the building on the other side,' Craig said.

Angie made a face, pulled off her hat, unlocked her car and tossed the hat inside. 'I hate wearing one of those things in the winter,' she said.

'Do you want to follow me round?' he said.

'Fine by me.'

'I'll go in Angie's car, since it's still warm,' Alex said.

'See you there.'

He walked over to his car and then Angie followed him out of the car park onto Tipperlinn Road. They turned left and drove along to the new part of the hospital, and parked next to each other.

'How do you know Olivia?' Alex asked Craig.

'Her father is a friend of my boss's, and he asked me if I would pop in to see her when I was coming up to Scotland. I was happy to oblige.'

'That's very good of you.'

'She's had a hard time of it,' Angie said, 'all because of a patient of hers.'

'Bastard. And Jimmy says she's been getting threatening letters.'

Angie nodded. 'We need to catch him.'

'The photo with the threat was from a killer I'm looking for in London,' Craig said. 'He just struck again, and I think he knows my movements and the photo was a message to me.'

'She won't be alone, Jimmy,' Angie said.

'That's good to know for when I go back to London. And I'll keep in touch.'

They walked into the hospital. In the reception area, a male nurse was waiting with Olivia.

'Well, it seems like we're having a party!' Olivia said, smiling.

The male nurse was a big guy, with tattoos on both arms. Craig looked at the design and thought maybe the tattoo artist had been pished when he picked up the needle, or else the nurse belonged to some obscure tribe on an island in the middle of nowhere. There was what looked like some Chinese writing on his arm. It could have said anything and the nurse wouldn't know. He might have been going for *spread the love* but actually got *fuck my sister*.

'Alright there, mate?' Craig said. The guy stood up and towered over Craig, a big guy.

'I'm not your mate,' he said in a Glaswegian accent, stepping towards Craig.

The DCI had been in many fights, and the secret, he knew, was not to back away. He didn't now.

'We're here now, son, so it's time for you to take a walk.' He made eye contact with the gorilla and there was something in the way Craig looked at him that made him look away.

Good choice, Craig thought.

'Shall we go for a walk?' Olivia said, smiling.

'You sure you'll be okay?' Gorilla asked, looking at Craig.

'I'll be fine, Leon,' Olivia said.

The nurse walked away without looking back.

'This is DS Alex McNeil,' Craig said. 'Her husband is DCI Harry McNeil. They're both more than willing to help you, Olivia.'

'That's great. Thank you.'

'And DCI Angie Fisher. She's come from Glasgow today. We spoke to your dad. He's concerned but happy you're making progress.'

'Nice to meet you, Angie. Thank you for coming along today. I'm getting there slowly. As each new day comes, I feel stronger. I'm even ignoring the photo and message I was sent.'

They ventured out into the cold, Craig walking next to Olivia, with Angie and Alex on either side.

'We can drive somewhere,' Craig suggested.

'I'd rather just have a walk into Morningside if you don't mind. I don't want to be too far away. It's like I'm on a rope, really, and this way, I still feel attached to the hospital.'

'Whatever you want is fine,' Angie said.

'When you're back in London, and Angie is back in Glasgow, will I still have friends to help me?' Olivia asked.

'Of course,' Alex said. 'Harry and I will help you, don't worry.'

'Thank you, I appreciate it. I promise you that I'll be able to go out on my own. It's just that I'm walking uphill just now, mentally speaking.'

'You'll soon be at the top, I'm sure,' Angie said.

They started walking through the hospital grounds towards the exit that would take them to Morningside. The place was getting busier as the day went on, with people doing their shopping on a Saturday, free from the constraints of the office.

They chatted as they walked, the three detectives ever vigilant. They reached Morningside Road, the cold wind shooting down from the top of the hill. It was busy with buses and cars and Craig wondered if this would be too much for Olivia, but she was holding her own.

She looked at the Canny Man's pub across the street. 'I haven't been in a pub in a long time. Back in the day when I still had friends, we would go out at the weekends, have a few drinks and a laugh.'

'Do you want to go in?' Craig asked. 'I'm sure they sell coffee.'

'I'd like that. Can we?' She looked at the others, and they nodded in agreement.

'Let's go,' Craig said, and walked by her side until they reached the pub. He held the door open, and Angie and Alex went in first, followed by Olivia and then Craig, like they were her protection detail, which, in effect, they were.

Inside, the interior looked old and was filled with antiques, some hanging from the ceiling, and theatrical props, making it a unique place.

Craig sat down with Olivia after giving Angie money to get them coffee. Alex followed Angie.

'When is Eve's uncle's funeral again?' Olivia asked Craig.

'Monday at lunchtime. There'll be quite a few uniforms there, but we can't get hold of his best pal, Mickey.'

'Mickey Thompson?' she asked.

'Yes. Do you know him?'

'I do. Mickey was a patient of mine when I worked in Fife. Obviously, I can't talk about him, but he was a nice man.'

'Somebody lamped him one, and now he's on sick leave because of his mental health problems. I think he should retire now. He and Clark were planning on doing their own thing when he retired, drinking and fishing, but that's not going to be happening now. I still think he should retire anyway.'

'He loved to fish and hike. He has a little place in Perthshire.'

'Nobody knows where it is. It must have bad mobile service because nobody can get hold of him to tell him about Clark.'

'I have the address,' Olivia said with a smile. 'I'm sure he wouldn't mind if I gave it to you. I'd have to look it out; it's in my little address book.'

'Have you been there before?' Craig asked.

'No, but he loved talking about it when he was in therapy. It's an isolated cottage. He's had it for ages. He and Clark would go up there all the time.'

Alex and Angie came over with four coffees and set them on the table.

'Thanks,' Craig said. Olivia smiled at them.

'Can I ask you,' Craig said, 'after you were taken

to the hospital after being attacked and you were no longer practising as a psychiatrist, what happened to your patients? I mean, I know many of them were investing their time with you and their lives too. They opened up to you and you became their rock. What happened to them?'

'My dad took some of them on.'

'That's a long way to go, from Fife to Glasgow, for some people.'

'That's why he did Zoom calls. They could talk to him from the comfort of their own home.'

'Do you know if Mickey Thompson used Zoom to talk to your dad?' Craig asked, not touching his coffee.

'Yes, he did. He couldn't talk about Mickey now that he was my dad's patient, but he did mention that he was taking care of him now, that I'd laid the foundations and he would continue. Nothing confidential was spoken about.'

'Olivia can't tell you about Mickey Thompson, but I worked with him. I can tell you about working with him,' Alex said.

Craig nodded. 'Just your personal opinion.'

'Yes.' She took a sip of her coffee. This part of the bar was quiet, so she could speak freely. 'Mickey Thompson is only a couple of years away from retirement. He's a good DCI, don't get me wrong, but you never knew which Mickey was coming into the office on any given day. I don't know what happened to him, but he had problems. DSup Mark Baker always cut him a bit of slack since Mickey was a good boss, but not everybody in MIT liked him. He could be all happy one day, like he'd taken some pills, and the next, he'd rip your head off. We saw him pacing about his office sometimes, talking to himself. He needed help. And I think he was getting it, and from what Olivia was saying, that help was coming from her father. But he could be strong-willed too. He said he had a lead from a CHIS and was going along to see if he could bring this guy in, and when we asked if we should go with him, he blew up. That's when he got smacked. But we think it was the mental health issues he has that got him sidelined for a little while. A lot of people think he should go out on medical disability, but I think that would mess his pension up.'

'Now he's at his little cottage somewhere,' Angie said.

'That's where he was going, Mark Baker said,' Craig told them.

'His little cottage in Dunkeld?' Olivia said.

'Yes,' Craig said.

'I do. He said I could use it any time I wanted, to just give him a shout and he'd get the key to me. I'm sure I still have the details written down somewhere. I didn't take him up on his offer.'

He looked at Alex. 'He doesn't have any family, does he?'

She shook her head. 'Not that I know of.'

'I think my wife's uncle was the closest thing to family he had,' Craig said.

Olivia's phone rang and she looked at the screen. 'It's my dad, checking up on me. You don't mind if I take it?'

The other three didn't mind. Olivia got up and walked along to the other end of the room.

'I'm in the Canny Man's pub with Jim Craig and another couple of detectives.' She looked at them and rolled her eyes. 'Of course I'm fine. I haven't been this fine in a very long time.'

She held the phone away from her ear, closed her eyes and jiggled her head from side to side.

'Okay, Dad. Come and see me soon. Bye.'

She walked back to the table and sat down. 'He thinks I shouldn't be doing this, but I told him it's long overdue. I can't be stuck in there for much longer. I need to be out and about.'

Craig nodded. 'I know this has been a long time

coming. Since I first met you years ago, I've seen you make excellent progress. We'll help you any way we can.'

'Thank you. All of you. But I'd like to go back now if that's okay.'

'That's fine by us,' Angie said.

'Absolutely,' Alex said.

They finished their coffees and got up to leave.

'Remember, though,' Craig said, 'err on the side of caution. The hospital shouldn't let anybody in to visit you unless it's one of us or somebody else you know.'

'I know, Jimmy. Thank you for caring.' Olivia put a hand on his arm and smiled.

He smiled back. 'Right, let's get you over the road.'

They left and it was just as cold as when they'd gone in, the wind still hovering about, waiting to ambush them.

'When do you think you'll want to go out again?' Craig asked.

'I think sooner rather than later. I'm slowly getting the old feeling back, that I want to be out and about again.'

'Call us anytime,' Angie said, taking up the rear this time.

'Thank you, I will.'

'Your dad isn't happy about you going out, I take it,' Craig said.

'He's an old fogey. He worries too much.'

'You can't blame him,' Alex said.

'Oh, I don't. I know how fathers can be. Protective of their daughters.'

They chatted about books – what Olivia was reading and what she recommended.

When they got to the door, it was spitting rain. They walked inside with Olivia and a nurse came, this time a female and not built as big as a brick shithouse like Leon.

'Call me anytime with Mickey Thompson's address if you find it, please,' Craig said to Oliva.

'I will.'

'Call us anytime, even just for a chat,' Angie said.

'Thanks for coming here today. I feel my confidence has been boosted.'

'Take care of yourself,' Alex said.

'Stick with it; you'll get there,' Angie said.

Olivia waved and the three detectives walked back to the two cars.

'I have to admit, I thought she would have been a lot more nervous,' Angie said. 'Considering she hasn't been out in a while.'

'She's a psychiatrist, remember. She was probably psyching herself up for this.'

'Well, whatever she did, it worked,' Angie said. 'I don't know if we'll meet again anytime soon, Jimmy, so if not, pleasure meeting you.'

'Same.'

Craig opened the door for Alex and then got in, putting the seat heaters on again. 'I'm at your mercy,' he said. She brought up his sat nav and typed in her address.

'I'll keep you right if the electronic female tries to take you the wrong way.'

Angie honked her horn as she passed and gave them a wave.

'Harry said he got called out because there was an explosion last night,' Craig said as he left the car park, turning into Myreside.

'Yes. A house was levelled, and it took part of the house next door with it. Other houses were damaged too.'

'Getting called out to a scene like that when you're MIT means they found a body and it looks like the person didn't die from natural causes.'

Alex laughed. 'I know. I worked at MIT.'

'Christ, sorry. It's how I explain things to my wife, even though she's heard it a million times.'

'It's okay, but you're right. I'll hear all about it from Harry when he gets home.'

'I hope Olivia finds her address book and can tell me where Thompson's cottage is. It's imperative that we find him.'

'You think he might be in danger?'
'I do. Very much so.'

TWENTY-FOUR

Craig drove away from Murrayfield, putting The Bridges in Dalgety Bay into the sat nav. He'd said hello to Jessica, Alex's sister, at the front door when he dropped Alex off. She said Harry and Alex's daughter was inside playing and invited him in for a coffee, but if he drank any more, he'd be whistling and crossing his legs halfway over the bridge. He did use their bathroom after the thought of stopping and pissing at the side of the road was too much.

It was late afternoon by the time he got home and Eve was upstairs in her uncle's old study. Finn barked and jumped around, pleased to see him, and held him hostage until he threw a ball a few times.

'What have you got going on?' he said, impressed

by Eve's hard work putting the newspaper clippings back up on the corkboards.

'It looks like Clark was obsessed with DS Stuart Hunt's murder.'

'Maybe because I was there and became family,' Craig said.

'No, I think it was more than that. He knew Stuart and his death hit Clark hard. The fact that the killer was in the wind and nobody ever caught him must have weighed on his mind.'

Craig looked at the various photos from the newspapers at the time. There were also hand-written notes and a photo of Hunt. 'I wonder if Mickey Thompson knew about this?'

Eve looked at him. 'I don't think this is the sort of thing Clark would have spoken to anybody about, do you?'

'I don't know. If he kept quiet about it, it was because he didn't have an answer. But then I think he did have suspicions, and if he voiced them, then that might have got him killed.'

'Have you spoken to Mickey Thompson yet?' Eve asked.

'That's the thing; we can't contact him. His phone isn't on, and we don't know where the cottage is. But Olivia does. She has the address written down in an address book and will try to find it and tell me.'

'Why would she have the address?'

'Because Mickey told her she could use it any time she wanted. He was one of her patients. You know, when he was struggling at times. He went to a psychiatrist and that happened to be Olivia.'

'She was his psychiatrist?'

'Yes. Then he started seeing Callum Strachan after Olivia was attacked. Strachan took over for her, so I'm assuming he had a few of Police Scotland's finest in his office.'

'Maybe he could give you a tune-up?'

'Hilarious. There's nothing wrong with this noggin.'

Eve's smile dropped. 'Seriously, though, I hope Mickey is safe. After what you think happened to Clark, there's no telling.'

'Let's not jump the gun, but I know what you mean. Clark, then Bert, Carrie's grandfather. And God knows how many more.'

'If he's not leaving any clues behind, like DNA or something, how will you catch him?'

'I'll ask Dan on Monday to search the system, looking for any reported sudden deaths in a house. I know we have the funeral, but afterward.'

'Come on. You hungry?' she said, ushering him out and putting out the light.

'I could do with a bite. How about a chippy?'

'Sounds good. Usual?'

'With plenty of brown sauce.'

While Eve went to call their order in, Craig called his son. 'Joe. It's Dad.'

'I know, Dad. Your name pops up on my screen.'

His son sounded stressed, but Craig couldn't blame the boy. 'I'm just calling to see how Carrie is after last night.'

'Shocked. I told her I'm here for her, but she feels numb.'

'I understand that.'

'It was a complete shock. She can't understand why the old boy went upstairs when there was no need to.'

Because somebody murdered him and wanted it to look like an accident. He didn't voice his thoughts, primarily because his only evidence was a lollipop in the old boy's trousers.

'Keep me in the loop, son. Pass on our best to Carrie. I'm assuming you'll still attend Clark's funeral on Monday?'

'I'll be there, Dad.'

'Thanks, son. I'll call you before that to work out the finer details.'

'Okay. Cheers, Dad.'

Joe disconnected the call.

When Joe ended the call with his father, Carrie Dickson was sitting on her couch. 'Christ, I don't know what I'll do without him.'

'It will be hard, Carrie, but I'm here. Whatever you need, I'll get it for you.'

The doorbell rang. 'You could start by seeing who that is and telling them to go away.'

Joe stepped out of the living room and answered the front door. He didn't recognise the woman, but a few moments later, he let her in. 'Sorry, but this lady says it's urgent.'

'Delphin! Come on in.'

The woman walked in, looking distraught.

'Joe is my boyfriend. Joe, this is Delphin, my granddad's cleaner.'

'Hi,' Joe said.

Delphin smiled at him. She turned to Carrie. 'First of all, I have to say how sorry I am to hear of your grandfather's passing. He was such a lovely old man.'

'Thank you,' Carrie said.

'I'm going to miss the fun we had.'

'He was a fun guy, even though he couldn't go on rollercoasters anymore,' Carrie said, smiling. Even into his seventies, Albert loved to go on rollercoasters when he got the chance. 'Please, have a seat. Do you want a cup of tea?'

Delphin sat down. 'No, thank you.'

Carrie indicated that Joe was making the place untidy and should also sit. He took a chair.

'I loved to listen to Albert's stories, especially the ones about when he was in the police force,' Delphin said, carrying on. 'He had so many tales, and lots of them about bad people. He was very brave. I don't know if I could do such things, like chasing a madman with an axe.'

'I'm sure he embellished much of it,' Joe said. Carrie shot him a look that suggested he was about as useful as a chocolate fireguard at that moment in time.

'Just saying,' Joe added in a low voice. 'I'll put the kettle on for a cup of tea.' He got up and left the room.

'He was a brave man, no doubt,' Carrie said, 'and

I'm sure he *did* embellish things sometimes, but when I was growing up, I used to love listening to him tell his stories about his days in the police. Of course, he was still in the force at the time.'

Delphin looked awkward momentarily, rubbing her hands together on her lap. 'I'm so sorry to have to bring this up, but I was coming round today anyway to pick up my money. I'm so sorry, but I'm making very little.'

'Oh God, no need to be sorry. This is your livelihood. I'm not sure where my chequebook is at the moment.'

'Albert usually keeps cash for me behind the clock on the mantelpiece.'

'Here it is, Delphin.' She passed it over to the cleaner.

'Thank you. I appreciated the work. Albert said he wanted to keep the house clean since you were at work all day, but honestly, I think he just liked the company.'

'Yes, he did.'

'We had much in common; I was also a police officer, many years ago. I did ten years but decided to change it up and went to work with the MOD Police.'

'Really? Granddad didn't say.'

'Oh yes, we chatted for hours about our careers. I was with Fife Constabulary, but I wasn't a detective like him. Our paths must have crossed at some time, but we didn't know each other. Funny that, how one time you meet somebody, not knowing you're going to meet later in life again. I'm so glad he wanted a cleaner.'

'You had your own business for a while now?'

'Ever since I retired from the MOD. A few years. I didn't want to sit at home twiddling my thumbs. I cleaned Clark's house too. I think he recommended me to Albert. It's not as exciting as being in the police, but it pays the bills.'

'That's terrific, Delphin.'

Delphin stood up. 'Thank you for this. And once again, I'm sorry for your loss.'

'Thank you.'

Carrie saw Delphin out just as Joe was coming back along the corridor.

'You didn't have to run my granddad down,' Carrie spat at him.

'I was just saying. She was in the police, she said, so I'm sure she embellished many of her stories when they were gabbing.'

'Just go, Joe. I don't want this to turn into a fight.'

He grabbed his jacket and went outside into the

cold. He thought he'd had more fun Saturday nights, then immediately regretted it. It wasn't Carrie's fault.

He started walking up the road towards his car, thinking that maybe this relationship had run its course. He had his head down against the cold when he bumped into someone.

'Oh, I'm sorry,' he said.

It was Delphin. 'Oh, it's you, Joe. I thought I was going to get mugged there for a moment.'

Joe laughed.

'I can't get my car to start,' Delphin said. 'It's round the corner. It's an old jalopy, but it usually gets me from A to B. I was going to ask Carrie if she had jump leads.'

'I don't think she would know what to do. But I can give you a lift somewhere if you like?'

'That would be a lifesaver. Thank you.'

TWENTY-FIVE

Sunday morning, the snow was still lying on the Fife side. Craig woke up with a splitting headache. He'd decided to have a few drams the night before, his head spinning from all the details of the murders.

After taking Finn out and having a shower, he sat with a coffee in the small sitting area of the living room, looking out to the sea. Finn came in to lie at his feet.

'Penny for them,' Eve said, bringing in a cup of tea.

Craig looked at his wife as she sat down next to him.

'Christ, Eve, I just can't switch off. I came here to help you with Clark's funeral, and I can't switch off being a police officer.'

'If you had, you wouldn't have figured out that Clark could have been murdered.'

'There. That's it. *Could* have been murdered. My dad could have been murdered. He was run off the road and when I went to look at his wrecked car, there was a lollipop in the passenger footwell. His girlfriend died in circumstances that, if you thought like a detective, could look like she was murdered. Carrie's grandfather was murdered, I'm sure of it. But if I went to the procurator fiscal, I would be laughed out of the office. Why? Because all I have is suspicions and some stupid theory about a lollipop being left at the scene. Nobody is going to believe that. I've had to convince myself for the last twenty-five years that the killer we were chasing held a lollipop stick to my eyeball, about to kill me with it.'

'Dan saw it; that must count for something.'

'It does, believe me, but he would sound equally daft if he told anybody that story.'

'Okay then, what about motive?'

'That I don't know. But what I do know from interviewing killers is that some of them don't need a reason. They're unhinged and they can't help what they're doing.'

'I'm a teacher, not a detective, but I've been married to one for a long time and it's rubbed off on me, listening to you talk about cases, so let me tell you what I'm thinking right now. I think this is personal.'

'What do you mean?' Craig asked her.

'He killed Stuart Hunt all those years ago. He tried to kill you, but he was interrupted. We went to London shortly after that. Now he's started killing retired coppers because, for some reason, they've been going over the Stuart Hunt case. Clark, Albert. You said your dad was murdered, in your opinion. What if he had suspicions? If you start asking too many questions, then you could be next. And that scares the shit out of me.'

'My dad would have gone to somebody if he had suspicions that he knew the killer. I think.'

'What about your mum?'

'No, she was dead before this started.'

'What about his girlfriend? What was her name again? The one who was in the car when he crashed.'

'Fran. Smith, I think it was. Fran Smith.'

'Would he have confided in her?' Eve asked.

'If I was a betting man, I'd have to say no. But you never know.'

'Maybe he did. After all, you think she was murdered too.'

'Who knows? He certainly didn't confide in me.'

'Maybe he was going to, but he was murdered before he could.'

Craig nodded. He realised that he hadn't known much about Fran Smith, back in the day. 'I'll do some research on Fran, on the Register House website. Maybe she has some relatives I can find and talk to.'

'I can do that today,' Eve said.

'Okay. I have to call Olivia again to see if she found the address of Mickey Thompson's cottage. I tried earlier, but her phone wasn't switched on.'

He stood up and Eve looked at him. 'What if it was a copper?'

He looked puzzled. 'Like who?'

She took a couple of breaths before answering. 'Mickey Thompson.'

Craig was silent for a moment, thoughts blowing through his head like a high-speed train. 'I'm listening, Eve.'

'He and Clark were friends. We know now that Clark had all that stuff on the walls in his study, but Delphin said it was always locked. Except for that one time when she looked in and saw the clippings on the wall. What if Clark was suspicious all this time? Not able to prove it, but it got the better of him, and he confronted Mickey. What if Clark had confided in old Albert, another retired cop? If Clark had confronted Mickey, then maybe that was enough to push Mickey over the edge.'

'This is all theory that we can't prove,' Craig said. Mickey Thompson had worked with his father, and Craig had known Mickey for the short couple of years he was on the force up here before moving to London.

'I know that. Hence the, "What if...?" Let me ask you this, though: have you been able to contact Mickey since you came here, to tell him about Clark?'

'No. His phone is switched off and nobody knows where the cottage is. Except Olivia.'

'Then maybe you'd better get hold of Olivia.'

He called her number, but it went straight to voicemail. 'No answer again. It must still be switched off. Maybe she's having a lie-in. It *is* Sunday after all.'

'Does she have a phone in her room?' Eve asked.

Craig shook his head. 'No.'

'Then call the hospital.'

'I will.'

He left the room, a bad feeling in his gut, the dog following him. He went into the dining room and sat at the table, Finn lying down beside him again. The master had moved, and since he wasn't doing anything exciting like throwing a ball, he put his head down.

Craig looked at his phone and played around on the internet until he found the number for the hospital. He didn't have it in his contacts since he'd always called Olivia's personal number.

'Hello, my name is DCI James Craig. I'm a friend of Olivia Strachan's.'

'Oh yes, I remember you, DCI Craig. How can I help you?'

'Olivia's not answering her phone and I'm trying to get hold of her. Do you think you could get a message to her?'

'I'm not sure to be honest. She left hours ago.'

'Left the hospital? Who with?'

'On her own.'

'Where did she go?'

'I think she said she was going to her house.'

'Her house?' Craig was confused for a moment, then he mentally kicked himself; obviously, Olivia had had a house before she went into the hospital.

'Do you have an address for her house?'

The woman on the other end hesitated for a moment. 'I'm not sure I'm supposed to give out that kind of information.'

'You know who I am, and I'm going to trust you

with some information too: I think she's in serious danger. And not from the man she's been hiding from all these years.'

'Oh my.' The woman took a deep breath. She told Craig the address.

'Thank you. One more question, then I'll leave you in peace.'

'Okay, go ahead.'

'How was she planning on getting up there?'

'She called a friend. She didn't say the name, but she said they were a police officer.'

TWENTY-SIX

'Christ, I think you need to watch the bacon sandwiches there, pal,' Craig said to Dan Stevenson as the big man plopped himself into the passenger seat of Craig's Volvo.

'I'm big-boned. That's what my mother used to say.'

Craig couldn't argue with that; Dan was a big guy, but he wasn't fat, despite Craig's insult.

'That's a myth. My mother used to say the same thing.'

'You're just a fat bastard, Jimmy, if you don't mind me saying.'

'I do, cheeky bastard.'

He pulled away from Dan's house as Dan was getting his seatbelt on.

'I appreciate you coming with me this morning,' Craig said.

'If there are any shenanigans, at least you have real polis with you.'

'I'm not sure if I've just been insulted or not.'

'You have, trust me.'

'I looked at a map earlier and looked at where Falkland is. Up the M90, along the A91, then down, or the A82 past Glenrothes and then up?'

'M90. Faster. You got blues and twos on this thing?'

'Aye.'

'Even faster.'

Craig made his way east to the M90 and then put the welly down, the siren and lights helping him get up the motorway as fast as he could. There was still snow on the hills and surrounding areas, but the road was clear, the spray lashing at the car's windscreen.

They made good time, the sat nav taking Craig exactly where he wanted to go.

'I don't know what the local traffic boys will make of a Londoner booting the bollocks out of his car with the lights and siren going if we get pulled over.'

'You can vouch for me, Dan.'

'Aye, watch me. I'll tell them I had a blackout and when I woke up, you were going off your nut, driving like you'd just stolen this.'

'Cheers for that, mate.'

'Nae bother.' Dan looked out the window, holding on to the grab handle above the door like he had just shat himself or was about to let one go, as Craig got onto the A91, cutting the speed back and turning the siren off.

'You've known this Olivia woman a while, then?'

Craig nodded. 'Aye. I visit her when I come up to Scotland. Long story short, her dad is friends with my boss and he asked me if I would, and I was happy to oblige.' He looked at Dan. 'I asked her if she knew where Thompson's cottage was, and she said she had the address in her address book. I didn't realise she would have to leave the hospital to find it.'

'And now she's not answering her phone.' Dan pointed for the Falkland turnoff just before the sat nav spoke up, and Craig made the right.

'Correct.' Craig turned off the lights as he headed through Strathmiglo, down the A912 towards the village.

He followed the directions until he came to a tight little street. There were no parking spaces in front of the houses, so Craig parked round the corner. In front of Olivia's house was an open area covered in snow. A war memorial stood tall, next to a cart that Craig assumed had been used in one of the wars.

'It's this one here,' he said to Dan as they stood outside. It was the first house in the street, stone-built and terraced. It had a white door with a black knocker, but they didn't need to use the knocker. Craig could see that the door was slightly ajar.

'Bit cold for keeping the door open,' he remarked, looking at Dan.

'That would certainly keep the heating bill high, right enough.'

They pulled on latex gloves and Craig pushed the door. It opened silently and just as he expected, the house didn't feel any warmer than the outside.

'Olivia! It's Jimmy Craig with a colleague of mine. Are you here?'

No reply.

Craig wasn't sure about the legalities of drawing his extendable baton, but if push came to shove, he would worry about it later. He walked further into the hallway. There was a narrow staircase straight ahead, the hallway stretching through to the back. There was a door on the left, slightly open, and Craig pushed it, keeping his baton over his shoulder, ready to bring it into action. He was glad to see Dan do the same.

He saw her in what was the living room, sitting on a chair facing away from him. The TV was on, playing but muted.

'Olivia?' Craig said. No reply. He took a step towards her, wondering if she had earphones in. He gave the chair a wide berth, which wasn't that wide considering the size of the room.

'Oliva?' he said again.

He coughed, trying to get her attention, but still she didn't move. He stepped round in front of her and only then could he see why she hadn't answered him.

TWENTY-SEVEN

Craig stood to one side, having no jurisdiction at this crime scene. Dan had called it in and the ambulance had arrived first, followed by a doctor.

'She doesn't look like she's been dead long,' he told Dan after he had pronounced life extinct. 'If I was to have a wee wager, I'd say her cause of death was blunt force trauma, if the trail of blood running down her face is anything to go by. But I don't want to put the pathologist's nose out of joint.' The doctor looked at Dan. 'Any idea which one of them is coming?'

'Dunfermline,' Dan said. Depending on the location and how busy they were, Olivia could alternatively have been taken to Kirkcaldy or Dundee, or even Edinburgh wasn't unheard of. But on this occasion, she was being taken to Queen Margaret Hospital.

'Professor Keller, probably. I heard she's on call today.'

'She's good.' The doctor tilted his head towards Craig. 'Who's your friend?'

'My name is DCI James Craig, London Metropolitan Police. Olivia Strachan was a friend of mine.' Craig said it in a *don't fuck with me* voice, and the good doctor just shrugged.

'Doctor Ian Short.'

Craig looked at him and nodded.

'Give me a call if you need anything else from me,' Short said to Dan.

'Will do, Doc, thanks.'

Short left the house just as Isla McGregor and DSup Mark Baker arrived.

'If I was a suspicious man, I'd raise my eyebrows at you two arriving together,' Dan said to Isla, Baker out of earshot.

'You are a suspicious man. You're a detective. And this is one coincidence that you'd better believe in.'

'Alright, alright, keep your knic...hair on.'

'What are you two sweetie wives talking about?' Baker said, his face flushed as if he'd heard Dan talking about him and was about to tear a strip off him.

'I was saying the doctor just left,' Dan said.

'Are you daft? I know he just left – we bumped into him when he was on the way out.'

'Oh aye. I wasn't sure you'd seen him.'

Baker held a hand out like he was speechless. 'Unless you see me coming in with a Golden Retriever and wearing sunglasses, assume I'm not blind. Deary me, you been on the lash this morning or something?'

'No, sir.'

He walked past Dan into the living room and Dan stuck up two fingers behind Baker's back.

'You do know the victim has a mirror above the mantelpiece, don't you, Stevenson?'

'I was just stretching my arm, sir.'

Baker ignored Dan as he pulled on a pair of latex gloves.

'Don't be touching anything now,' a man said, coming into the room, all white-suited but not booted. He had the hood pulled up and was carrying a bag of his equipment.

'This is not my first rodeo, Stan,' Baker said, tutting.

'Yet here I am, the only one who's in the proper

gear.' The man looked at Craig. 'I don't believe we've been introduced. Stan Mackay.'

'DCI James Craig. Jim. I'm not here in an official capacity.'

'Good meeting you, Jim,' Mackay said then Craig left the house. Dan and Isla followed.

He blew a breath into the air. 'Fuck's sake. I wish to God I hadn't asked Olivia to find the address of Mickey Thompson's cottage. I thought she had her address book with her in the hospital. I didn't realise she'd kept her house after she admitted herself. She should have told me and I would have come up here with her.'

At that moment, a car pulled up at the end of the street behind the police vehicles. A woman got out from behind the wheel and went to the boot and rummaged about inside, before coming out with a large bag.

'Professor Annie Keller,' Isla said. 'From Queen Margaret Hospital. She drives like she wants to be found upside down in a ditch one day. You would think she would want to drive a Porsche or something. Make cutting her out of the car a little more interesting.'

'An Audi isn't bad. Those things can shift. And with all-wheel drive too.'

'Put your eyes back in your head, Dan, you're a married man,' Isla said. Then to Craig: 'You can't blame yourself for what happened. This was out of your hands.'

'The person I spoke to at the Royal Edinburgh said Olivia was being picked up by a police officer.'

'Mickey Thompson?' Dan said.

'They don't know.'

'Christ. We need to get round to his house and see if he's there. We can get a warrant,' Isla said.

'Based on what? Suspicions and conjecture?' Craig said.

'We should still go round there and have a look.'

'Yeah, we could do that. There's nothing else we can do here. The pathologist and the crime scene guy will want us out for a while.'

'Besides, Baker's in there, strutting around,' Isla said.

The woman approached them, a cigarette between her lips, her bag in one hand and a white suit over the other arm. She put the bag down on the snow and took the cigarette out, blowing smoke into the air. 'Thank Christ. I've been needing that, but my own rule is no smoking in the car.'

'I hope you're going to suitably dispose of that

before entering the crime scene, Annie,' Stan said from the doorway of the house.

'I don't know how I would cope if you weren't around to guide me, Stanley.'

'I'm an angel sent from heaven. Somebody's got to look after you. Those things will kill you.'

'The detectives or the cigarettes?'

'You're a doctor too. I bet you've cut up people with better lungs than yours.'

'At least they don't lecture me on my smoking.' She took another drag before nipping the end and making it disappear. 'Besides, I don't lecture you on eating doughnuts.'

'Well, I've cut back to just twenty a day. Oh wait, that's what you always say.'

'It's down to ten now, Stanley. Can't you tell?'

'From your wit and humour disguised as sarcasm? That must have slipped by me. See you inside.' He turned and disappeared back into the house.

'He's a peach.'

Craig saw she was a good-looking woman who looked after herself. She could be in her late forties or maybe early forties; it was hard to tell.

'Professor Keller, this is DCI James Craig, up visiting from London,' Dan said.

'Pleased to meet you, DCI Craig.'

'Likewise. Call me Jimmy, please.'

She gave him a surprised look. 'I was expecting a more southern accent.'

'I started my career with Fife, but then I transferred. Born and bred here.'

'Just visiting, or...?'

'My wife's uncle died. We're here for the funeral and to make other arrangements.'

'Sorry to hear that, Jimmy. Call me Annie. Everybody else does because there's no respect for authority anymore. Isn't that right, Dan?'

'Yes, Annie.'

'See? I'd better get inside. I see the forensics van is here and Stan's crew is hovering around waiting for me to finish.'

'He seems to have forgotten the pecking order,' Dan said. 'Captain Y-fronts is in there too.'

Annie nodded. 'DSup Baker been getting on your wick again, Dan?'

'He caught me sticking the vickies up behind his back.'

Isla shook her head. 'His wife can spot a blonde hair on his collar in a darkened bedroom at two in the morning, but he can't spot a mirror on the mantelpiece. Maybe his wife should be the detective.'

'Caught again? I've told him that Dracula is the only one who can't see anything in a mirror.'

'I'm right here. I can hear you both,' Dan said.

'He'll never learn,' Isla said. 'I told him to make sure DSup Baker is well out of sight before sticking the vickies up.'

'It's not sticking them up behind his back if he's already moved out of range, is it?' Dan pointed out.

'This is true. Well, you have at it then, big man,' Isla said, slapping his arm. 'I'll get the door-to-door started while you go and check out Mickey Thompson's place.'

'You don't think Mickey's a goner as well, do you?' Annie said.

'It's more complicated than that, Doc,' Dan said, his face suddenly serious.

'Right. Don't tell me any more. I'll take my kit inside and get changed in there.'

'See you around,' Dan said.

'Nice meeting you,' Craig said to Annie.

'You too.'

With that, Craig walked away with Dan. 'She seems...like the life and soul.'

'She is. Give her a few voddies and she's off.'

They got to Craig's Volvo, and he took one last look at Olivia's house and they got inside.

After the car was running and they left the scene, he made a phone call.

Angie Fisher answered on the third ring, and Craig pictured her fighting to get the phone out of her back pocket.

'Jimmy! How are things going?'

Craig felt the words stick in his mouth before he spoke. 'Angie, Olivia's been murdered.'

'What? How the hell did that happen?'

'She came up to Fife to her house in Falkland. I didn't know she had kept it on. She was up here looking for an address book. I thought she had it in the hospital with her.'

'Oh God, Jimmy, that's awful. I'm so sorry.'

'I think maybe DCI Mickey Thompson is clearing house now, Angie. I think he's been killing for years.'

'You still don't know where this cottage is?'

'No idea.'

'Keep me in the loop, Jimmy. Anything you need, just give me a shout.'

'Thanks, Angie, I will.'

He ended the call.

'Listen, Jimmy,' Dan said, 'I know this isn't protocol, but Olivia had a little address book on the table at the side of her chair, and I flipped through it and took some photos. The address you're looking for was in there.'

'Where was I when you were doing this?'

'Checking the rest of the house. I was going to mention it when you came back down, but you wanted me to call it in, and then you went outside for some fresh air, and then one of the neighbours came along and...well, long story short, I have the address here. It's just outside of Dunkeld.'

Craig stopped the Volvo on the main street where Falkland Palace was. 'We can either go to Thompson's house in...where?'

'Kirkcaldy.'

'Kirkcaldy. Or we can boot it up to Dunkeld. Kirkcaldy is closer, but there's a chance he's been hiding out in Dunkeld.'

'I can have Isla go to Kirkcaldy. With half a dozen uniforms.'

'Aye, do that. And if she happens to smell gas when she's there, have some big bastard use his size thirteens to take the fucking door off its hinges.'

'I'll call her,' Dan said, then put the Dunkeld address into the sat nav.

Craig floored it.

TWENTY-EIGHT

'Christ, Joe, where are you?' Eve said to herself, hitting the 'end' button on her phone. Once again, her son wasn't answering his phone, which was typical when he was hungover.

Maybe he had spent the night with Carrie. She needed to talk to him about the funeral tomorrow, and she didn't want to leave it until the last minute. And now Jimmy was away looking for Olivia.

She put her jacket on and took Finn outside. It was cold and the snow wasn't in a hurry to leave, but it made the place look nice. She'd always liked her uncle's house, enjoying the view down to the flats at St David's Harbour, and the bridges. It was a million-pound view without the cost.

Finn did his business, and she took him back

inside. He'd been fed earlier, so he was good to go. 'Lie down, baby,' she said, and he went over to his blanket that was on the living room floor near the window. He wasn't allowed on the bed during the day and he would be quite content there.

She went downstairs, got into her Volvo and headed along the coast to Kirkcaldy.

She got a strange feeling every time she came back to Fife. Memories of growing up here, of her own family, now all gone. Her dad would take her down to the links in Burntisland to go on the rides and eat candyfloss before walking along the promenade. She'd play on the beach with her bucket and spade with her friends while all the adults were having a good time.

She missed Fife so much. London had become grotty and filthy and wasn't a good place to live anymore. And when Rose had told her that a teaching position had opened up, it had made Eve feel more unsettled than ever before. She was going to run it past Jimmy, to see if they could come back to Scotland. She was sure that Joe would want to stay up here too. But she had asked her husband to follow her when she went to work in London and he had followed her, transferring to the Met. Would he come back up north with her? She hoped so, even though it was a big ask.

She thought it was because she was getting older, this feeling of longing. It would have been stronger if she had any other family here, but Joe was the pull. They could sell their house in London and live here. She hadn't told her husband that she'd heard from the solicitor and that Clark had left everything to her, including the house they were staying in just now. All it would take was a signature and it would be theirs. They wouldn't have to hunt for a house to buy because they had one.

The thought excited her: being near Joe; having a job, if she applied and got it, but Rose had assured her that she would walk into the job.

She took the coastal road, looking out over the sea to Edinburgh. It would be nice driving over there for a night out or getting a train and having a few drinks. She couldn't think of anything better, but what if her husband said no? What would she do then?

Her mind was on her new life when she pulled up outside Carrie's house. She walked up to the door and knocked. No answer. She stood back and looked at the upstairs windows. The curtains were still drawn. Maybe she and Joe were in bed. God, she hated the thought of that, her son just sleeping around with young women. That was the old-fashioned Eve, but the here-and-now mother told her that this was the twenty-first century.

'Are you looking for Albert?' a voice said. She looked over to her right. An old woman was standing at her open doorway.

'I know Albert passed. I'm looking for his granddaughter, Carrie.'

'You'd better come in for a cup of tea then.'

TWENTY-NINE

They stayed on the main A9 for as long as possible. The snow was heavier up here, the hills covered in it, but the road had been well-maintained.

'I don't know what the side roads are going to be like,' Dan said, looking out the passenger window. 'Probably shite.' He looked at Craig. 'Just as well you've got this Swedish mobile.'

'You're making me wish I had a Chelsea tractor now.'

'Or just a tractor.'

The female voice told Craig he had to take the next right, onto a smaller A road. This had been ploughed, but it wasn't as good as the main road. They drove for a few miles, the road getting more winding the further they went.

'Look, there's Loch of Craiglush. I didn't know they had named a loch after you,' Dan said.

'You're hilarious, Dan. Maybe we'll come across one named after you: Loch Heid-the-Baw.'

Dan laughed. 'That was a stretch there, even for you.'

'I know. I'm ashamed the words even came out of my mouth.'

Further along, they passed a gated driveway to some steading, with a small gatehouse. A No Entry sign told them they couldn't come in unless it was for some event.

'I've always fancied a gaff like that in the country,' Dan said. 'Bit of peace away from the wife and kids, although my daughters are adults now. Still, a wee bit of relaxation now and again wouldn't hurt. What do you say, Jimmy? Does that idea ring your bell?'

'Not for me, pal. I don't need to drive miles away up some lonely road to enjoy myself.'

'You're not scared, are you?'

'What? Away. Behave yourself. The first thing I'd do is get a licence for a shotgun.'

They drove on and came to a small village called Butterstone, the sign telling them to drive safely.

Craig turned left onto an even smaller road that

still had snow on it. The Volvo took it in its stride as they climbed higher.

'God's own country,' Dan said, looking at the snow-covered hills. They took it slowly for another few miles until the sat nav told them they had reached their destination, which was a track with an open gate.

'Hang on to your wig, I'm going to boot the bollocks off this thing to try and get us up there,' Craig said, stomping on the accelerator. But no matter how good the all-wheel-drive system was, it didn't want to go up the snow-covered track, and the car slid sideways.

'Just as well we brought our wellies,' Craig said. 'I told you it would be shite up here.'

'What do you mean *we*? I have boots on, but they're far from being wellies.'

'I always keep a pair in the back in the winter,' Craig said. 'Sucks to be you.' He got out into the biting wind, opened the boot, and swapped his regular boots for his wellies.

'I hope you know you look like a bloody farmer with those things on,' Dan said, pulling his beanie on.

'Nope. You can't wear them. Besides, your feet

are so big, they would feel like stilettos to you.' Craig closed the rear hatch and locked the car.

'I don't want them anyway,' Dan complained. 'My wife has a pair like that, just so you know.'

'Couldn't give a shit.' Craig started walking up the track, Dan beside him.

'You come all the way up from London and you end up working a busman's holiday. You must love your work, Jimmy.'

Craig stopped. 'This is personal, remember?'

'Aye, you're right.' Dan looked straight ahead. 'What are you looking at?'

'The driveway. There are no tyre marks, like nothing has driven down it since the snowfall.'

'Which means that Mickey Thompson already left before the snow fell overnight.'

'You called Isla about going to his house in Kirkcaldy, didn't you?' Craig asked.

'Yes, I did. They should be there now.'

Craig started walking, his boots sinking into the snow, which was about six inches deep. 'If we go in here, at least that's the two places we know of that he owns being checked.'

The climb up the track would have been hard enough but was doubly so with the snow covering it, but they made good time. Turning round to the left, they climbed higher, and eventually the cottage came into sight.

Craig looked around him; the hills in the distance looked spectacular covered in snow, and he could see why Thompson had wanted to buy this cottage. If peace was his thing, then he had chosen the perfect spot.

The sky was grey and held the threat of more snow.

They approached the cottage, and as they got closer, they could see a parking spot, but no cars were there. The cottage had been built with one storey, but there were dormers in the roof, suggesting rooms had been added upstairs. It was well kept, and Craig could imagine Clark enjoying the peace up here.

'Any idea what kind of car Thompson drives?' Craig asked.

'A Volkswagen Golf.'

Craig nodded. 'I'm assuming that Isla knows that too?'

'I think so.'

'When we get mobile reception, call her and ask her to get the team to look around the area for it.'

They walked up to the door, Craig aware they

could fall into a trap. The front door was open, not wide, but wide enough to have let the snow in.

Craig nudged it with his foot. The interior was cold and he could see the snow hadn't been disturbed. He stepped over it, looking at Dan and indicating for him to check the ground floor. He approached the staircase straight ahead and started to climb. This looked like it had been added to access the rooms above and it was narrow, with only room for single beds to make it up to the next level. Furniture would have had to be brought up piece by piece and assembled in situ.

He started to smell the odour before he was all the way up the stairs. The unmistakable odour that every copper around the world knew.

He stopped when he got to the top and saw an open door. It led into a bathroom with a huge dormer that had been built onto the back.

Two more doors, both shut. Craig didn't bother with stealth now. Just because the car wasn't out front, that didn't mean the house was empty, so he kicked the first door, assuming somebody might be inside. The room was empty, as was the freestanding wardrobe. The curtains were drawn, keeping the room in the shade.

He quickly left that room and went into the next

one, and that was when he saw the blood on the bed. Lots of it. The curtains weren't drawn in this room, like somebody wanted whoever came in to immediately see the mess. Craig stepped over to the freestanding wardrobe and opened it, the smell hitting him even harder.

Inside the wardrobe, in a sitting position, was Mickey Thompson. The wounds in his chest were massive, and his gut was hanging open. His skin was pale and waxy-looking.

'Dan! He's up here!' Craig shouted. He heard the thump of Dan's feet on the stairs. 'In here.'

Dan burst in looking like he was about to go boxing, until Craig pointed to the wardrobe.

'Jesus,' Dan said. 'He looks like he's been dead for a while.'

Craig nodded in agreement. 'He certainly didn't kill Olivia.'

'Then who did?'

'The person who took his car.'

'We need to call this in.'

'We need to get back down towards Dunkeld first, where there's reception. Let's go.'

THIRTY

DCI Mickey Thompson lived on a street off Kirkcaldy's Esplanade, a minute's drive from the sea.

Isla McGregor got out of her car, and seven officers bailed out of the police van – the biggest bastards from Police Scotland they could muster at short notice.

A uniformed sergeant walked over to her and stood looking at the semi-detached villa. 'Nice place. See what climbing the ladder will get you, Isla?'

'I'd settle for a nice wee place in Spain, to be honest.'

'Seems like Thompson liked his wee getaway up north. Have you heard from Dan yet?'

Isla looked at her watch. 'Not yet, but the reception is a bugger up there.'

'Right, let's do this.' He turned to the other six men. 'Shock and awe. And don't take any shite from him because he's a DCI. He's a bad bastard by all accounts.'

'Allegedly,' Isla said.

'Allegedly,' the sergeant repeated. He walked up to the front door and turned to face the men. 'You three, get round the back.'

The three officers ran off, going up the driveway to the back of the house.

Isla stepped forward and opened the letterbox. 'Just for the record, I think I smell gas,' she said, letting the flap go and standing back.

The sergeant grinned. 'Right, get that door in,' he said to the nearest uniform. The young man raised his foot.

'For fuck's sake, it's a UPVC door, ya bawbag. I meant with the enforcer.'

'Oh, right.'

Although the sergeant had no doubts that the big lad would have ripped the door from its frame, he wanted this done right. The big lad took the red metal enforcer used for breaking down doors and skelped it a few times until the lock burst, and he shoved the door as it bounced back, and then they were in.

The living room was on the right and there was a bedroom on the left. One uniform ran through to the back and unlocked the door there when he saw the key in the lock.

There was a set of stairs over to the left, and Isla went up with the sergeant, while some of the others went through the house, two uniforms following them.

'The place is empty,' she said after they'd gone through all possible hiding places.

Then her phone rang.

It was Jimmy Craig.

'Hi, Jimmy,' she said.

'Isla, call off the search before you enter the house.'

'Too late. We took the door off its hinges.'

'Okay then. We found Thompson dead in his house. He's been dead for days, looks like. Look and see if you can see his VW Golf outside.'

'Oh Christ. I will. But that means that somebody else killed Olivia. Have you any idea who would want to do that?'

'Not yet. Dan and I are coming back. We won't be long.'

'See you when you get here.'

THIRTY-ONE

But Craig wasn't going back to Kirkcaldy.

'Where are we going, boss?' Dan said.

'Back to where it all started, Dan. Back to where you saved my life.' Craig looked at the DS. 'Falkland. Where we've just come from.'

Once again, he booted his car down the road, the tyres hissing on the tarmac as the AWD kicked in. To give Dan his due, he might have been shitting a brick at the speed Craig was doing, but he didn't say a word.

When Craig got close, he drove by the old woodworking school and the house to its right, then pulled off the road onto a smaller side road. 'Go and find Mark Baker. I'm sure he'll still be at the Olivia crime scene. Call Isla.'

'What are you going to be doing?'

'I'm going into that house. Where we found Stuart Hunt dead. It's the only place that makes sense, and if the killer isn't there, then we'll get our heads together. But go and let somebody know where I'm going.'

'I'm not letting you go in there yourself.'

'You have no choice.' Craig opened the driver's door and stepped out, followed by Dan, who walked around the car.

'This doesn't feel right.'

'Go, Dan. It's five minutes away.'

'Oh shite.' Dan jumped in behind the wheel and adjusted the seat. Then he turned the car around and headed back to Falkland.

Craig walked down the road. The snow made the place look brighter than it normally was under the canopy of trees. He crossed the road, trying to keep low, and then the house where the killer had been going to ram a lollipop stick into his eye appeared behind the snow-covered vegetation. The main house was a short distance away, and obviously the years hadn't been good to this old house, which had fallen into complete disrepair. The roof was gone, having fallen into the main body of the house many years ago, so Craig knew the killer wouldn't be hiding in there. He had to be in the main house, where Stuart Hunt had been found murdered.

He could also have been in the woodworking school, but Craig had seen it in the distance, and it too looked boarded up. He'd check the house first.

Still shielded by the snow-covered vegetation, he approached the house. It was set back from the road a bit, and there were bushes and vegetation between the road and the house itself, as well as the tall trees creating a canopy over the road. He supposed all the greenery would offer some kind of protection from the road, but it wasn't a main road anyway, and no cars had passed since Dan had left with the Volvo.

As he moved into the bushes, snow falling on him, he saw the VW Golf parked outside the house, and now he could get a better look, he saw smoke rising from one of the chimneys.

He knew he had come to the right place.

He made his way through the bushes, and cut directly across the back garden, his feet hindered by the deep snow. Anybody looking out now would see his footprints, but that couldn't be helped. Nor did he care. Olivia's killer was in this house and he was going to take the bastard down.

He approached the back door of the house and tried the handle. Many people who lived in the countryside didn't believe in locking their doors, and the owner of this place was of the same opinion.

He tried to be quiet, but the wind was kicking up and it blew some snow in. He quickly shut the door behind him and walked out of the kitchen, along a hallway towards the living room. He could hear crackling coming from what sounded like a log fire.

The interior of the house was well kept and it was obviously lived in.

The living room door was at the bottom of the stairs, and after looking up quickly and seeing nobody there, he pushed the door gently, hoping the hinges wouldn't squeak. They didn't.

The house was warm and there was a roaring fire in the fireplace, flames dancing around the logs, spitting fire and sparks.

The room was sparsely furnished, with a small couch under the front window, and a chair next to a lamp and a bookcase.

But it wasn't this that caught Craig's attention.

It was the two people sitting over on his left, gagged and tied to wooden dining chairs.

Joe and Carrie.

'Christ, Joe!' Craig said, stepping towards his son. And then he realised he had made a fatal mistake, ignoring something he had been taught in training.

He hadn't checked behind the living room door.

A figure stepped out from behind it and smacked him on the head with something. Craig fell on one knee, his eyes swimming for a second. He looked around, unable to make out who it was at first, but then his vision cleared and he saw the killer he had been looking for.

And thought at that moment in time that he and his son were going to die on the same day.

THIRTY-TWO

Eve drove her Volvo like she was possessed. It had been a long time since she had been in Falkland, the last time at a wedding years ago, but she knew where it was and how to get there. She knew where the place that her husband had told her about was, recounting the events of that night many times. To get to it, she had to drive right through Falkand and stay on the main road.

As she was heading out of the town, sure she was heading in the right direction, she saw her husband's car speeding towards her, but it wasn't her husband driving. It was a big man. Craig had talked about Dan Stevenson a lot in the past few days. Why would Dan be driving Jimmy's car?

Going to get help? Surely he wouldn't leave

Jimmy behind? Unless her husband had issued explicit instructions for Dan to go and get help.

Christ, where had he come from? It had to be the old woodworking place Jimmy had often discussed. Clark had told her about it too, about how her husband had nearly been murdered by a serial killer there, one who had got away and whom they had never caught.

The killer who had come back and killed Clark for getting too close.

Where was this place? she wondered as she slowed down. Then she saw it, an old sign pointing to a road on the left. She jammed the brakes on, signalled left and turned in.

She just hoped she wasn't too late.

THIRTY-THREE

'Delphin,' Craig said, standing up on shaky legs. He looked quickly at his son, who had gaffer tape over his mouth and his hands tied behind his back. Carrie was the same; her eyes were wide and she was making noises behind the tape.

'Why did you poke your nose into things, Jimmy? You should have left things well alone. Now I'm going to have to kill you for real this time.' She smiled and took a lollipop out of her pocket. 'This one's for you. I won't ram it into your eye, though. I'll kill you and just leave it in your pocket.'

'That was you, all those years ago? Why?'

'Yes, it was. I'd been in uniform for ten years by that time. I was passed over by CID a few times, and I knew it was cronies like Thompson and Mark

Baker and even your father who were stopping me. I knew I was better than any of them. Brighter and sharper, more intelligent, but that wasn't good enough for them. Because I was a woman. I wasn't in their inner circle.'

'That was in the late nineties. That sort of thing didn't go on back then. Maybe in the seventies, but not the nineties.' Craig's head felt like it had been rammed into a brick wall.

'You think so? Jesus, shows just how much you know. I was being rejected before you even joined the force! I overheard your father saying that you would walk into CID when you did your time in uniform. Nepotism! It was ludicrous. That's why I started killing. It came easily to me. My father was a nut job, and it's in my genes. And as I suspected, they couldn't catch me. They came close, on the night you almost got me. Then that big oaf came charging along and I had to decide: kill you and get caught, or just run. It was your lucky night, Jimmy.'

'You left a lollipop at each murder scene, right?'

She laughed. 'Yes. And it was brilliant. I knew they were there, but nobody else did. I was leaving my signature behind, but nobody ever figured it out.'

'Why a lollipop?' Craig asked.

Her face changed then. 'Because one of those

bastards said I'd make a better lollipop woman than a detective.'

'I found Mickey in his wardrobe at his cottage.'

'Good for you. It was a long time coming. I should have done it years ago.'

'Why did you kill him? Was he getting close to finding out you were the killer? Just like Clark and Albert?'

'Mickey didn't have a clue. Unlike Clark. He had his suspicions and had those newspaper clippings on his wall.'

'Why did you tell me about them?' Craig asked.

'I just didn't want you to find out and wonder if I knew and why I hadn't told you, so I gave you some cock-and-bull story about him leaving his study door open and me seeing them. I mean, I can't even be sure Clark knew, or was even close to finding out, but I couldn't take the risk.'

'How long were you in uniform?' Craig asked her, shuffling a couple of steps towards her. She didn't budge or tell him to stop.

'I left shortly after the night I almost killed you. Then I went to the MOD Police and worked down in Rosyth. Then when I retired, I started my own cleaning business and made sure I bumped into Clark one day and told him about it. He took me on because I was cheap. Same with Albert. I wanted to get into their homes and start befriending them, getting them to trust me. Keep an eye on them.'

Then it came to Craig, the answer to the nagging question he'd been asking himself since he'd been to Olivia's: why was her house so clean?

'You cleaned Olivia Strachan's house.' More steps towards her.

'Yes, I did. I know her father. I got talking to him and he recommended me.'

'Is that why you sent him and Olivia the photos of the hammer? Pretending you're the killer I'm investigating in London?'

Then he moved forward in a flash and grabbed her arms. 'You're under arrest for the murder of DCI Mickey Thompson,' he said, and she did something unexpected. She laughed.

Then he felt his legs being kicked out from under him and he fell for the second time, rolling onto his back. He looked up at his son.

'Joe?' Craig looked his son in the eye and saw him smile after he ripped the tape off his mouth. 'What are you doing?'

But Joe didn't answer. He merely reached down to the side of the fire and picked up a hammer. And brought it back up above his head.

THIRTY-FOUR

'Don't you fucking dare!' a voice screamed from the doorway. Eve stood looking at her son.

Delphin took a step towards her. Craig stuck his leg out and tripped her up and she went sprawling. She yelled just as Eve caught her by the hair and yanked her head back.

'Go on, Joe, do it! Let the bastard have it!' Delphin shouted.

Joe grinned. 'I'll do it in my own time.'

'You'll do nothing of the sort! I don't know why you're doing this, but you'll put the hammer down,' Eve shouted.

'He's not going to listen to you,' Delphin said, her hand trying to grasp Eve's.

While Joe was distracted, Craig jumped to his

feet and put himself between his son and his wife. His head was still splitting, but that was the least of his worries.

'What the hell are you doing, son?' Craig said to Joe.

Delphin laughed. 'But he's not your son, is he? He's mine. Flesh and blood. You only adopted him.'

Craig looked at her from the corner of his eye, not taking his attention from Joe. 'He's our son, mine and Eve's.'

'I gave birth to him! He's mine! *He* came looking for me! And I was glad to welcome him home. Not like his father.'

Eve pulled Delphin's hair tighter.

'Ow. Let me go, bitch.'

'Let her go,' Joe said.

'Drop the hammer,' Craig said.

'You'd like that, eh?'

'I would. Then we can talk.'

'There's nothing to talk about.'

'I think there's plenty!' Craig shouted. 'Like why you're here, with a serial killer, and why you have the hammer in your hand.'

Delphin laughed now as if she was oblivious to the pain. 'I met him in London, five years ago, when he was sixteen. He contacted me and I went down. I saw so much rage in him. I think he got that from me. He was angry with you, Jimmy. Successful copper, yet you never had time for him. It was the job. He thought you were showing off after you caught killers. Just like I felt with Mickey Thompson and the others! I showed Joe how to channel his anger, and he made his first kill with the hammer.'

Eve's eyes were wide, but she kept Delphin in front of her.

The colour dropped out of Craig's face. 'You're The Hammer?' he said to Joe. 'The killer I've been hunting? I don't believe it.'

'Believe it, Jimmy boy. I knew you wouldn't catch me. I'm too smart for you. I even killed Olivia. She was the easiest one.'

'Why didn't you just come to me if you were upset with me?'

'Why would I want to talk to you? I hate you,' Joe sneered. 'You adopted me when I was two. I never bonded with you. Either of you.'

'How could you be down in London killing when you were up here at university?' Eve said.

Joe laughed. 'That shows how much you pay attention; I dropped out after the first semester.'

'You were going down to London to kill people

with a hammer?' Her voice was starting to crack now.

Craig looked at the young man he used to know as his son and knew he had lost him forever.

'Why Carrie? Why did you bring her here?'

'Last night, Delphin –'

'Mother,' Delphin corrected, and Eve yanked her hair harder.

'Mother approached me in the street and told me her car had broken down and I was going to give her a lift. Just in case any nosy neighbour was looking out. But then Carrie came out and started poking her nose in. So we just took her in the car. Believe it or not, I wasn't going to kill her. I like her. Now I'm going to take my hammer to her.' Joe turned to look at Carrie and her eyes went wide.

'I'm not going to let you do that,' Craig said.

'Really, old man? I don't think you have a choice.' Joe rushed at him, swinging the hammer, but Craig caught his arm. Joe dropped the weapon but fought like a wild animal, punching his father. Craig rolled with it but fell. He held on to his son, pulling him over, but Joe got up and kicked Craig.

Eve screamed and pushed Delphin into Joe, and they both staggered but they didn't fall. Delphin rushed back at Eve, but she sidestepped and brought the palm of her hand up, connecting with Delphin's chin.

The woman fell onto her back and then sat up. 'I'm going to fucking kill you,' she said to Eve.

Then Joe did something that Delphin wouldn't have bet on in a million years. He hit her on the top of the head with the hammer, killing her instantly.

'Now, where was I?' he said, smiling. 'Oh yes, I'm going to kill you all.'

He turned to Craig, who was lying on his back, extreme pain threatening to close him down before the hammer did.

Joe took a step towards him, raising the bloodied hammer.

Then all hell broke loose. The front window in the living room exploded. Joe turned to look at it just as Dan rushed into the room, taking Joe down in a rugby tackle.

The hammer went flying and Eve kicked it out of the way. Craig got to his knees, held on to his ribs and threw himself down on Joe's kicking legs.

Isla ran in and helped the men get Joe's arms behind his back and handcuff him. Then the room was filled with uniforms and finally, Joe was overpowered.

DSup Mark Baker came in as the uniforms stood Joe up.

'I'll see you again, *Mummy*!' he shouted.

Dan helped Craig to his feet. 'Twice! Twice I've saved your arse. Drinks are on you, pal.'

'I'm never going to live this down,' Craig replied, then saw Isla holding his wife as she started crying uncontrollably. He went across to her and put an arm around her. He didn't know what to say.

'I saw the mirror on the wall this time,' Dan said to Baker. 'So no vickies.'

'And yet you still don't see a Golden Retriever.' Baker shook his head. 'How in the name of hell will we write a report about this?'

THIRTY-FIVE

It was raining when they got out of the car in the cemetery in Dunfermline, more akin to October than December. Craig had woken up that morning stiff as a board, but the doctor had told him this was to be expected with three broken ribs. Every time he winced, he thought of his son kicking him. He looked around at the faces, still expecting to see Joe in the crowd, but he knew he was in the secure unit in Edinburgh.

The first doctor who had examined Joe had told Craig and Eve that he believed that Joe had dissociative identity disorder. One minute he was asking for his mum and dad, the next he was like a raging psychopath.

Craig put up his umbrella over himself and Eve.

She put an arm through his as they walked with the other mourners towards the grave.

Isla fell into step beside Eve. 'I'm here for you. Like I said, I'm not married, I have plenty of time on my hands and I'm here to help you through this.'

Eve smiled. 'Thank you, Isla.'

Dan took up a position beside Craig. 'Likewise for me, big man,' Dan said.

'I appreciate it, Dan.'

Baker brought up the rear, holding his umbrella. Dan fell back from Craig's side.

'Can I get under your umbrella, Mark?' he said.

'Nope. The amount you'd need to cover your giant noggin, I'd be soaked.'

Isla fell back with her umbrella. 'Here, jump under mine,' she said.

'You're spoiling him, Isla. It would teach him to remember his own in the future.'

'That's fine, Mark.'

'Never let it be said I didn't warn you.'

The service was well attended, despite the weather, the mourners coming up to Eve and Craig and offering condolences, none of them aware that their son was now in custody.

Back at the house afterward, there was a small gathering. A couple of Clark's neighbours had rallied around, ensuring the caterer was there on time and taking Finn out. The dog was happy to see everybody.

Craig was standing by the window, looking out over the sea, when Eve came up behind him.

'Are you going to apply for the job?' he asked her.

She looked puzzled for a moment.

'Rose told me,' he explained. 'She just happened to mention there was a vacancy coming up.'

He had a glass of whisky in his hand, and not the first one by the look of him, Eve thought.

'Take it if you get the chance. I was thinking of putting in for a transfer back up here,' he said.

'You were?'

He nodded. 'Down there, I'll forever be the detective whose son was the serial killer he was hunting. I'll be lucky if I'm directing traffic. No MIT officer will trust me. If I can't transfer up here, I'm leaving the force. But I already ran it past Mark Baker and he said it took a lot for me to take down my son. And catch your uncle's killer. He'd be happy to have me on the team, now there's a vacancy for a DCI.'

'Don't you feel like you'd be jumping into a dead man's shoes?'

'Not really. Mickey Thompson hid it well, but he was a bad bastard, by all accounts.'

'If that's what we both want, we should do it. Besides, I still want to be near Joe. He's going to need us now more than ever.'

Craig drank some more whisky. 'He'll never get out; you know that, right?'

'I know.'

Dan came over, a glass of whisky in his hand. 'I hear you're planning to transfer back up, Jimmy?'

'Did Mark tell you?'

'No, I was eavesdropping.'

'Fair enough. Yes, we're both thinking of coming home.'

'Good for you. It's just that the last time I saved your life, you skipped off to London before you had a chance to take me out for a pint.' He smiled at Craig.

'Don't worry, I'm sure there will be plenty of nights out, Dan. This time I won't disappear for twenty-five years.' Craig nodded. 'I'm coming home and I'm going to stay this time.'

'Good man.' Dan left in search of food.

'Where will we stay?' Craig asked Eve.

'Before the funeral, I had a call from a solicitor in Dunfermline. Clark left us everything. The house, his car, even the money he had stashed away in the bank. It's all ours. We can live in this house if you like.'

Craig looked out over the water again before looking back at his wife. 'I think I'd like that very much.'

AFTER WORD

I hope you enjoyed the first installment of my new series, and thank you for coming along on this inaugural James Craig novel.

Thanks to Jacqueline Beard who has a better set of eyes than me! Thanks also to Lisa McDonald and to Gary Menzies for letting me use his name. And to my family, my greatest supporters.

If you could see your way to leaving a review or a rating, that would be really helpful. Thank you in advance.

If you want to contact me, please do. Go to my website and use the contact button there and I'll get back to you as soon as.

AFTER WORD

www.johncarsonauthor.com

Stay safe my friends.

John Carson

ABOUT THE AUTHOR

John Carson is originally from Edinburgh, Scotland, but now lives with his wife and family in New York State. And two dogs. And four cats.

www.johncarsonauthor.com

Printed in Great Britain
by Amazon